M. F. S.

Legends of the Saints

M. F. S.

Legends of the Saints

ISBN/EAN: 9783741195686

Manufactured in Europe, USA, Canada, Australia, Japa

Cover: Foto ©Andreas Hilbeck / pixelio.de

Manufactured and distributed by brebook publishing software
(www.brebook.com)

M. F. S.

Legends of the Saints

LEGENDS OF THE SAINTS.

By M. F. S.,

AUTHOR OF "STORIES OF THE SAINTS,"
"STORIES OF HOLY LIVES," "CATHERINE HAMILTON," "CATHERINE GROWN
OLDER," "TOM'S CRUCIFIX AND OTHER TALES."

London:
R. WASHBOURNE, 18 PATERNOSTER ROW.
1876.

CONTENTS.

vi CONTENTS.

CONTENTS.

LEGENDS OF THE SAINTS.

LEGEND OF
THE MOUNTAIN FLOWERS.

IT was early morning—so early that the moon had scarcely set, and a few faint stars still glimmered in the sky—when a little peasant maiden left her home to search for flowers to deck the village church upon its festival day.

Bright blossoms grow in the gardens, fragrant roses and sweet white lilies; the

2

meadows are gay with bluebells and daisies;
yet Annette will have none of them. It is
to the mountain she is hastening, for she
thinks that the flowers which grow nearest
to God and heaven must surely be the fittest
offering to lay at the feet of Jesus that day.
The big stones cut her little naked feet, but
she heeds not; the priest has said that the
smile of the Divine Child will rest on the
fairest gift, and to win that smile Annette
toils on as the day breaks and the first
golden beams of sunlight rest on the mountain top. At last she reaches the rocky
path, which scarce any foot can tread,
higher still, where only the wild goat tra-
verses; yet no flowers can she see; but
above her, on the mountain top, there is
one pure white blossom ; she climbs there
and secures it, and one, too, of the heaven's
own blue which grows by its side. One

more—she *must* have one more to offer to the Holy Child—ah, there, in the midst of the briars, a delicate rose is growing. The sharp thorns pierce her hands, and the blood from them stains the petals of her flower; but she has it safe, and her task is done.

"Annette, Annette, show me those fair sweet flowers," cries a clear voice, and there on the rock is a lovely child, with eager eyes and arms outstretched, and such a golden light in his long hair that Annette could almost fancy a glory is around his head. "Give me those flowers," he said again; but the little peasant girl shook her head, and, smiling, answered,—

"I cannot; I cannot. They are to offer to Jesus to-day in our village church."

But the little one begged still harder. "Let *me* give them to the Holy Child," it

2 *

said, and as Annette hesitated, it turned away tearfully.

" Stay, stay, little boy; you may have my flowers; you may give them to the Holy Child," but as she held them out, one bright drop fell from her eyes in the centre of the blue flower and rested there.

In the little church the village children are clustering, bright flowers are laid at His feet, but as yet Jesus has bestowed no smile upon them.

Annette is there, with bowed head and swimming eyes. She alone has made no offering to the Holy Child that day.

But a sweet soft voice speaks her name, bidding her look up. The child of the mountain is there, with the golden light around his head, and three blossoms are in his little hand: the lily of faith and the emblems of hope and charity. Ah! the child of the mountain was indeed the Holy Child, and Annette has now His smile as He clasps to His breast her flowers—the flowers which grew so very near to God and heaven.

LEGEND OF
THE COUNT AND THE LEPER.

THERE was once a rich and noble Count who, although he had great possessions, counted them as nothing for the love of the Lord Jesus Christ, and for that love he delighted to serve the poor and suffering, knowing that thus he was indeed serving his Master. He would even wash and tend lepers with the greatest charity, visiting them in their poor cabins; and one of these who dwelt near his castle he went to see every day, getting down from his horse and going in to wash his feet and give him an alms, and then departing. After some time the Count was absent for a while from his home, and during that time the poor leper died and was buried.

Some days after, the Count returned to his castle, and his first care was to mount his horse and ride to the cottage where he had so often visited the poor suffering man. Dismounting, he entered and found the leper there as usual, so that he joyfully performed his work of mercy and then went home, saying to his servants, "It has given me such happiness to visit my leper to-day."

The servants gazed at him in surprise, exclaiming that the poor man had died, and was buried during his absence from the castle; yet the Count continued to protest that he had washed the feet of the leper according to his custom, and that he was lying on his bed as he had been always before.

However, it was at last proved to him that the sick man was dead. They took him to the place where he was buried, and showed him the empty bed, and then the Count rejoiced, for he knew that he had been permitted for once to minister in person to his Lord as a reward for serving Him so long in the person of His suffering servants.

LEGEND OF
THE CHILD OF MAYER.

MAYER, the rich burgomaster of the town of Basle, had a little lovely son of two years old, who was laid low in dangerous sickness.

Day after day the parents watched anxiously by the child's side, hoping and praying for his recovery ; but, instead of reviving, their little son grew worse, and human aid seemed of no avail.

One night the burgomaster was watching

alone by the sick child : it seemed indeed as
if each hour must be his last.   As the time
passed on the little one never stirred, but
lay so motionless that ever and again the
father drew closer to make sure that still he
breathed, and at last, throwing himself down
beside the bed in an agony of grief, he cried,
"Oh blessed Mother! thou who hast a
parent's heart, thou who hast felt a mother's
sorrows, pray for us, pray for our child. Grant
that this precious little life may be spared
to us ; but if it be the Will of thy Divine
Son that he should die, then, O Mary, pray
that his sufferings may be shortened, for
they are more terrible than we can bear."

For a time the strong man knelt there
sobbing like a child ; but at last he rose,
and sinking upon the chair where he had
sat to watch so many a weary night before,
he listened again to the hour chiming forth

from the cathedral spire. At last it seemed to him that the door opened, very gently, very softly. There was not even the sound of footsteps, and yet as he raised his heavy eyes the Blessed Virgin, with her Son in her arms, stood within the room, a long blue mantle falling round her figure, a crown of gold upon her head. The graceful form glided silently past him and up to the child's bed, then placing the Infant Saviour on the ground by Mayer's knee, Mary raised the sick baby in her arms.

Was she going to bear it away then? Had the answer to his prayer been heard so very quickly, and would those terrible sufferings thus end at once? This was what the burgomaster asked himself as he sat still and silent, full of wonder at the holy vision.

But the Mother of Jesus did not bear away the sick child. Ah, no! she held him

tenderly in her arms, and smiled so sweetly
on him that the boy opened his long-closed
eyes and gazed wonderingly at her. Then,
with a marvellous gentleness, she laid him
once more upon his bed, and taking up her
Holy Son glided from the room as noise-
lessly as she had entered it. When morning came, Mayer saw that his little child
was saved. Its breathing was regular, its
skin moist and cool, and it knew its parents
again when they bent over it, and stretched
out its arms as it lisped their names.

Oh, how great was the joy of that household! They had dreaded the coming of
that day lest they should find the child
had passed away in death, and they poured
forth eager questions as to how the wondrous change had come.

Then Mayer told them of his prayer, told
them of the Blessed Virgin's visit in the

stillness of the night, and how his child was healed by resting in the arms which had clasped her own Divine Son. So, to mark their gratitude, and in remembrance of the favour God had granted them, Mayer had a picture painted of Our Lady holding in her embrace his suffering child, the Infant Saviour standing by her side; and thus her gentle compassion is recorded to this day, for that memorial hangs in the Picture Gallery of Dresden, to the praise and glory of her whose heart was touched by a father's tears and prayers.

LEGEND OF
THE PRISONER'S CHAINS.

A YOUNG man named Theodoric was taken prisoner during a war in which he was engaged as a soldier, and he was cast into a dungeon within the walls of a gloomy castle.

After a while, having promised to pay the ransom which was fixed as the price of his liberty, Theodoric was moved from the dungeon into a room, and here he remained, being fastened with iron rings around his feet and manacles round his arms, which were attached to a chain and thus fixed to the wall.

Six servants were placed as a guard over this young man and the other prisoners, who watched them narrowly by day and by night. Before he slept, Theodoric always invoked the Blessed Virgin and his patron saints; and one night after doing so he dreamed, and it seemed that in vision he saw himself seated upon a horse, still chained by the arms and feet, and yet two of his own kinsmen were by his side, who said to him, " Do not go, for our Lady of Kaisersbach has set you free."

At these words he awoke, feeling great joy, and scarcely knowing whether what had happened was true or whether it was indeed but a dream, and as he pondered over it all, he moved his fingers to one of his feet and touched the wearying, galling chain he had worn so long. Wonderful miracle! it fell from him without any difficulty, and so did the chain from his hand. Many a time before, he had tried to loosen his fetters, but in vain; now with a touch they were gone; but unfortunately the noise of their rattling roused one of the servants, and as he looked sharply round, Theodoric, in terror, tried to slip the chain upon his arm. However, it would not go on; long as he had worn it during his imprisonment, it seemed now too short and small; so he felt still more sure that he had been freed by a miracle, through the merits of Christ's most Blessed Mother; and keeping perfectly still he raised his heart in prayer for help, and the servant soon fell asleep again. He still had the chain fast to one foot; but he managed to rise softly, and getting to the window let himself down by a cord. After a while the same servant awoke once more and found the prisoner had escaped: an alarm was given, and men, blowing horns, pursued him in all directions. Many a time they were almost upon him as he crouched behind some thicket of trees; many a time their dogs nearly discovered him hiding in the brushwood; but Theodoric was in the keeping of Mary, so nothing could harm him.

One morning, in the early dawn of day, the young soldier knelt before the altar of the Blessed Virgin in the Monastery of Kaisersbach, to return his thanks for her merciful assistance in setting him free from his long captivity; and there he laid the chains which had been loosened by a miracle, as a continual acknowledgment that it was to her he owed his escape.

LEGEND OF
THE MONK AND THE BIRD.

T was summer-time, and the sun-shine brightened the dark green leaves of the forest trees, under the shade of which a monk walked slowly, his thoughts turned to God, and his lips moving in whispered prayers. A book was in his hand, and as he opened its pages and read, in the words of St. Augustine, of the unseen beauty of heaven, he said, "Ah, my God! I believe; but I do not understand."

As the words escaped him the monk suddenly heard the sweetest singing, and gazing upward he beheld a snow-white bird, which sang amongst the branches in thrilling notes of surpassing clearness. Closing his book he listened with a look of rapture upon his face as he seemed to see in vision the heavenly city, and hear the feet of angels softly treading its golden streets. He would have caught the lovely bird, whose song was of the city of God, but it escaped him and flew far, far away over hill and dell; and as he heard its notes no more, he observed that his own convent bell was ringing for the hour of noon. Quickly he retraced his steps, but to his amazement the familiar faces were all changed : new forms filled the oaken stalls, new voices chaunted

3 *

the Office; and yet it was the same old convent, the same cloister, the same quiet chapel.

"Who art thou?" asked the prior. "By thy habit thou are one of our brethren, and yet during the forty years I have been prior I never saw thy face."

"My reverend Father," replied the monk, "it was but this morning, at the hour of prime, that, with permission, I left my cell, and in the quiet of the wood I listened to the melodious singing of a strangely beautiful bird, until the bell called me home in haste, for it seemed that instead of hours I had but heard those thrilling notes for a few brief moments."

"Hours!" exclaimed a very aged monk, who sat upon an oaken bench against the wall, one so old that he had been there longer than all, serving God by prayer and penance for a whole century. He remembered the features of Felix, and added: "It is years since thou didst leave thy convent: for an hundred summers back I was a novice in this place, and there dwelt here a monk who bore thy name."

Then they searched in an old brown book, wherein were written down the names of all who had ever been in that holy house, and in it was recorded that upon a certain day the monk Felix had gone forth from the convent at the hour of prime, and, never more returning, had been counted among the dead.

Then they all began to understand how in listening to that celestial song the years had seemed as moments, and Felix, falling upon his knees, bent his head humbly before his Lord, and murmured, "Ah, my God, now I understand that in the beauty of Thy heavenly city and the joy of Thy presence, a thousand years are but as a moment, and time is no more known." Thus saying, the monk bowed his face to the earth and died.

LEGEND OF
THE WHITE THISTLE.

HE long hours of darkness had begun
on one of the weary nights when
the Virgin Mother and her Holy Son were
flying with S. Joseph into a strange land.
Shivering with fatigue and cold, Mary could
go no further, but sank down upon the sand
of the desert, with the Divine Child still
clasped in her arms. At length S. Joseph
discerned a cleft between two large rocks,
which would be some shelter from the cold

night wind; and, having laid a mantle upon the ground, he placed the Virgin and Jesus there to rest.

At the foot of the rock a little flower was blooming, a lowly humble thing that scarce a traveller would have heeded — a flower of a bright red hue. But that night, during the silence and stillness, when the only watchers were the gleaming stars in heaven above, Mary rose to give nourishment to Jesus, and as she nursed Him— singing a sweet low hymn to soothe Him to sleep—one drop of her milk fell on the lowly little flower which bloomed at her feet. From that moment its rosy hue fled for ever, but it was fairer and lovelier by far, for the little thistle had grown white as snow, and has so remained to this very hour, in remembrance of the night when Mary and the infant Jesus rested so very near it.

LEGEND OF
THE MASS OF THE HOLY CHILD.

A TERRIBLE pestilence was desolating the fine old city; in each street there were some dead and some dying, and neither Mass nor fast nor prayer seemed to stay the disease. One morning, when the sun gilded the spires of the ancient ivy-covered church, the priest stood ready vested, waiting to offer up the Holy Sacrifice; but, although he had rung the bell, no footstep was heard approaching; there was not even a server to attend upon him at the altar, and his heart was cast down under a burden of sorrow.

"O God, have mercy upon this city! Have mercy upon the lives of Thy people," he prayed. "Must it indeed be that no Mass shall be offered to Thy praise and glory this day? O God, forbid that this should happen!"

Even as he knelt in supplication, the priest saw that lights were ready burning on the altar, and a wonderful sense of the Divine Presence filled his soul as a strain of music thrilled through the building and a figure advanced from the sacristy dressed in white of dazzling brightness, having a face of angelic beauty such as man never had.

The heavenly server knelt by the side of the priest, and the Mass began, while music from angel voices echoed through the aisles until they died away into softest silence at the " Ita missa est." All was over : the heavenly visitor had vanished, and the priest knelt long in thanksgiving after that wondrous Mass which had so filled his heart with awe and reverent love ; and when at length he left the church, the news greeted him that the plague was abating, that the stricken people were recovering, for the Sacrifice which had been offered at the altar that day had stayed God's hand and spared the ancient city.

LEGEND OF ST. CHRISTINE.

IN the little town of Tiro, on the borders of the Lake Bolsena, there was a Roman patrician, an idolater, whose daughter had embraced the Christian faith. One day as this maiden, Christine, stood at her window she saw many poor and sick begging; and, to her great distress, she had nothing to give them. Suddenly she remembered that her father had many idols of gold and silver, and, being filled with pity for the sufferers,

she took these false gods and, breaking
them up, distributed the fragments amongst
the poor. When her father returned and
found what she had done, his fury was terrible, and he ordered his servants first to beat
her with rods, and then to cast her into a
dungeon. But in her captivity angels from
heaven came and visited her and healed her
wounds.

Then her father ordered that a millstone
should be tied round her neck, and that she
should be thrown into the lake; but the
angels still watched over her, so that she
did not sink, but floated on the surface of
the water ; and God, seeing what Christine
suffered for His sake, sent a still more glorious angel to conduct her safely to land.
Then her father cried, " What means this
witchcraft ?" and commanded a furnace to
be prepared, into which she was thrown ; and

there she remained five days, unharmed, singing the praises of the Almighty. Next the order came that she should be dragged to the temple to be sacrificed to Apollo; but no sooner had she looked upon it, than the idol fell down, and her father's terror was so great that he died on the spot. Then the Governor Julian, hearing that Christine, in her prison, sang ever the praises of God, commanded his soldiers to cut out her tongue; but, behold! she sang sweeter than ever, and the serpents and foul reptiles which shared her dungeon became harmless as doves. So the angry governor had the maiden bound to a post, while arrows were shot at her until she died; and thus Christine at last won her martyr's crown and was carried by the angels to heaven.

A LEGEND OF THE ROSARY.

IN the sunny land of France, in fair Provence, there dwelt a little orphan girl, who the simple peasantry called Mary's own child, because they believed that all little ones who have no earthly mother's care are specially watched and shielded by the Blessed Virgin.

The girl grew up amidst the woods and fields; she learnt from no books, her only books were the pictured windows of the old church, which showed each mystery of her Blessed Mother's life, and there, day by day, the child knelt before the shrine of Our Lady, and at her feet would say her rosary.

Once it chanced that she was very weary; so weary that she threw herself upon her bed, forgetting all about her rosary as she fell into a heavy sleep.

But she was soon aroused by a wonderful light in the little room and a sweet perfume as from the blossoms of numberless roses, whilst a lady stood close by her bed, so fair and beautiful, that the child felt sure she did not belong to earth, and by the twelve bright stars with which she was crowned, and by her blue mantle, she knew that it must be her Mother Mary.

Then the child knelt before her with folded hands and downcast eyes; she had seen that upon Our Lady's robe there were wreaths of roses in a beautiful pattern, but in one place it was not perfect—just a single rose was wanting!

But Mary's sweet soft voice addressed the girl: "My child," she said, "this rose-wreath, so fair and fragrant, is what your love has twined for me from day to day; but how is it that for once your work of love has been undone? how is it that you have forgotten to say my rosary to-day? Surely *you* will not be unfaithful. There are so many in the wide world who forget me and forget my Son, but I cannot spare your love," and then the vision was gone, while the child bowed her head with shame, and large sorrowful tears trickled down her cheeks.

Never again was the rosary forgotten by the girl—day after day she said it, no matter how sorrowful or weary; but from that time

4

she seemed drooping slowly, like a flower that fades in the garden—it was as if that vision of her gentle Mother had been a glimpse of heaven and she could linger in the world no more. So, very soon there was a small grave, which pilgrims to Our Lady's shrine go and visit, and are told that the child was laid there whom Mary herself taught to say her rosary.

LEGEND OF
THE KING'S DAUGHTER.

THE fair young daughter of a great king walked one day in the gardens of her father's palace, gathering the flowers all wet and glittering with dew, and as she plucked them and held them in her hands, she began to wonder who it was that had made these lovely blossoms; and she thought He must even be a greater king than her own father, and she wished that she could see His gardens, for they must be still more beautiful than her own.

In the middle of the night, when the king's daughter lay upon her bed, it seemed as if a voice called to her from the garden, and, after hearing it once or twice, she rose and opened the casement. There, in the moonlight, she beheld the figure of a most beautiful youth whose feet were hidden in roses, and she went down to the door and held it open for him to enter. Then he said: "I am the Master of the flowers. I come from the garden of Paradise and from My Father's home, for thy sake, because thou didst desire to know Me. If thou wilt follow Me, I will give thee a garland of crimson roses." As he spoke, the heavenly visitor drew from his finger a ring of pure gold, and he asked the maiden if she would be His spouse and give all her heart to Him, and she replied that she would very gladly do so; and as she said this she saw that there were wounds within His hands, and a still deeper wound at His Heart, and as the blood began to flow from them she cried out: " Oh, my Love, what does this mean? Thy Heart and hands are red with Blood!"

Then the youth smiled sweetly upon the maiden, and said : " It is for thee I shed this Blood; it is for thee I bring these roses; they come from the Cross whereon I died for thee." Then the young princess doubted no more, but followed Him at once to His Father's home. Thus shall we, if we, too, long to see and know the Lord of heaven and earth, hear some hour His sweet Voice calling us to leave all and follow Him, and He will lead us safely to one of the mansions of His Father's kingdom.

LEGEND OF
THE ROBIN RED-BREAST.

IT was a terrible day. Never since the world was made has there been a time so sad and awful as that of which I tell you, so very long ago.

The sun gave no warmth or light, the whole world was dark and gloomy, because a cross had been carried up the steep mountain called Calvary; and nailed to it, with a thief on each side of Him, Jesus, the Son of God, hung bleeding and dying.

Many people were gathered there, some to look and wonder, some to mock and revile; others, but these were few, to weep and sorrow for the cruel sufferings they could not hinder; and there was one, the Blessed Mother of Christ, who knelt at the foot of the Cross clasping it tightly with her trembling hands, while the tears streamed from her eyes, and her tender heart was pierced with anguish, because her Son — whom she had nursed as a little babe in her bosom, and loved so fondly as her child as well as her God—was dying that painful, cruel death.

A little bird came fluttering round the rugged Cross, a little brown - feathered creature, and it knew that its Maker hung there, pierced with the long nails, crowned with the sharp thorns; and the tiny robin was sad because it could do nothing to spare one pang of the many which were borne so patiently by Him Who created it.

So, at last, the bird flew away from the terrible sight—away to a garden not far off, the Garden of Gethsemani, where so lately the Lord Jesus had suffered His cruel agony, alone in the stillness of night, when all the world—even His own disciples—were sleeping.

The robin perched on a branch of one of the trees and gave a little melancholy cry. The wind swayed the branch roughly to and fro, as it will do before some threatening storm, and the bird trembled with fear, and it could not rest, but flew back once more to the mountain and the blood-sprinkled Cross.

"Ah! if I could but do something to help my Lord," sighed the robin; "if I could but bear some little pain instead of Him, how happy should I be. But I cannot. I am only a poor, feeble, frightened little bird, of no use to the God Who made me."

So it flew round the Cross once more, close, very close, to the head of the dying Saviour, nearly fluttering against the thorny crown ; and then it thought of something it perhaps might do.

"If I could but draw out one thorn from that piercing crown, it would only be a little thing, a very little thing to do ; and yet, surely it would be worth trying to give my Lord one thorn less to pain Him. He would not know it ; but I should like to do that, because I love Him so."

So the little brown robin flew near, and slowly, and with difficulty, it drew one long sharp thorn from the aching, bleeding head ;

and as it was fluttering away, bearing its burden in its beak, the dying Saviour raised His eyes and saw what the love of the bird had done for Him.

"Because you have pitied Me and sorrowed for Me," He said, "you shall bear always upon your breast the mark of My Blood, so that in time to come, when men gaze upon you they may remember how you came to Me and tried to help Me when I was dying on the Cross."

So ever afterwards the breast of the robin has been tinged with red as a remembrance and reward of that little service of love done by a tiny bird for its suffering Creator.

LEGEND OF
OUR LADY OF GUADALOUPE.

STRANGERS had been amongst the Indian tribes, strangers who showed them no mercy, who drove them from their dwellings like hunted deer; and there was none to help them, for when they called upon their heathen god he did not heed their prayer.

But holy men came through the forest-paths, who told them of God and the Blessed Virgin, and taught them to live as

Christian men. One of the noblest of the
race made his dwelling there; he learned
each tale the Fathers told of Mary, and every
week he journeyed to the nearest city to
hear Mass in her honour. On his way he
passed a hill where a heathen temple had
once stood, and there he would always pause
and sing the litany of the Blessed Virgin,
that the evil spirits might be put to flight
if they still lingered there.

Once, while singing the praises of Mary
on that hill-side, he heard sweet strains
mixing with his own—strains so sweet that
he felt sure they came from no voice of this
world—and then, in the midst of dazzling
light, a figure stood before him whom he
knew to be the Queen of men and angels.

"I know thy love for me," she said,
"therefore I bid thee take a message to
the chief of the holy Fathers : say to him

that I will have thee raise a church upon this spot where I stand, and none shall invoke me here in vain."

The Indian hastened to the Bishop. He spoke of the vision he had seen and of the desire of his glorious Mother; but the Father's words were cold and stern: "It is a wondrous tale," he said; "but I dare not think it true."

Again the chieftain heard the singing on the hill-side, again he saw the dazzling light, while the sweet voice spake to him: "Hast thou performed my will?" it said; and, bowed to the ground, he could only tell her it had been in vain; his message was not believed.

" Seek thy priest again," said the vision; "bid him, if he loves me, attend to my request." And the Indian went; but the Father only smiled: "Thou hast done what

was bidden thee; go in peace," he said.
Sadly and sorrowfully the Indian went
homeward.   Our Lady stood before him
once again, asking him of his success, and
then she bid him return to her on the
morrow, when he should bear a sign to
the Bishop from her.

He went. The Blessed Virgin appeared,
and, smiling, bid him bring her flowers from
the hill-side, and with these she twined a
fragrant wreath, which he should bear to
the good Father, in token that the vision
was true.   The Indian wrapped his treasure
in his cloak, and took his way through the
city, where he sought the Bishop.

" See, my Father," he cried, "our Blessed
Mother has sent to you a sign," and as he
spoke he threw back the folds of his cloak.
Ah! no flowers are there, no half-faded
wreath, but the face of the Virgin Mother!

drawn as though by angels, before which the Bishop bent his knees in reverence. Multitudes came flocking to see that wondrous sign, and there, upon the hill-top, a church was raised, in which there was an altar to Mary, blazing with gold and rarest gems, given by the chief of the Indians; and the cloak with its marvellous likeness was preserved as a sacred relic of the Mother of God, whose praises are sung by many thousands of Christian pilgrims to that spot.

LEGEND OF S. THOMAS.

THE Lord Jesus Christ once appeared to S. Thomas the Apostle, when he was at Cæsarea, and said to him: "The King of the Indies seeks for workmen who shall build him a finer palace than can be found even in the city of Rome. I send thee to him."

So S. Thomas went, according to the command of Christ, and received the order of the King to build him a palace of great magnificence, and much gold and silver was given him for that purpose. For two years the King was absent in a distant country, while S. Thomas, obeying a secret inspiration from God, instead of building a palace, set about distributing the treasures he had received among the poor and sick; so that when Gondoforus returned and found nothing done he was full of indignation, and ordered that S. Thomas should be seized and cast into prison, while he should decide upon some way of putting him to death. Meanwhile the King's brother died, and a marvellously beautiful monument was about to be erected for him; but after four days the dead man suddenly arose, and sat upright, and addressing Gondoforus, said: "The man whom thou wouldst torture is a holy servant of God. I have visited Paradise, and there the angels showed me a rich

5

palace of gold and silver and precious stones, and they said, ' This is the building which S. Thomas has erected for thy brother.' "

When the King heard this, his heart was touched with sorrow for his anger and revenge, and he himself hurried to the prison that he might deliver the Apostle. Then S. Thomas said to him: " O Gondoforus, dost thou not yet know that those who desire heavenly things care little for the riches of earth ? In heaven there are many mansions of wondrous beauty, prepared from the beginning of the world, for those who purchase the possession through faith and charity. Thy riches may prepare the way for thee to such a palace, but they can never follow thee there."

LEGEND OF
THE KNIGHT OF TRATZBERG.

THERE was once a Knight of ancient time who neglected even his religious duties, because his whole mind was given to the pleasures of the chase, and thus he lived from year to year in forgetfulness of God, Who had created him. He could risein the early dawn of morning at the sound of the huntsman's horn, but in vain the chapel bell invited him to holy Mass; and though day by day it fell upon his ear, he refused to rise to adore God, and even tried to cover his head with the bedclothes, so that he might not be disturbed by the tinkling sound of the bell.

One day his guardian angel seemed in a special way to force the thought of his duty into his heart; but the Knight was obstinately deaf to those gentle pleadings, and rolled himself still more warmly in his downy coverings, with a feeling of contemptuous pity for those who, though they must work hard all the day, still gave that first half-hour to obtain God's blessing at the Holy Sacrifice.

The bell ceased ringing. Although he strove to turn his mind to other things, the Knight seemed as if he could not help picturing to himself the worshippers in that little chapel, the good priest at the altar, the humble peasants kneeling and telling their sins, their sorrows, their cares, to Almighty God ; yet he resisted the good impulse which led him even then to rise and join them before the solemn moment of the consecration. " I will not," he said, and, turning on his bed, tried still more to think of his usual amusements and pleasures.

The Mass went on ; the little server-boy upon the altar bent lowly before his Lord as he rang the three-fold bell, which told of the sacred mystery which had been accomplished, and the chapel bell rang out the joyful news to those who were lying upon sick beds, and could only unite their intention and prayers with those who were present at the Holy Sacrifice. The Knight heard it upon his easy and luxurious couch—but in a moment a shrill and piercing cry escaped him, a cry which rang above the sudden sound of the rocks rattling together under the stone walls of his strong castle, making it shake and tremble.

The people rushed from the chapel to his room, alarmed by that shriek of anguish ; but, to their horror, they beheld him dead upon his bed, while upon his throat remained the marks of three black and burning claws. For many a year after there were marks upon the wall, which were said to have been sprinkled by his blood ; and generation after generation have told the history of this Knight, who resisted the pleadings of God's Holy Spirit, and was at last overtaken by His awful judgments.

LEGEND OF S. CHRISTOPHER.

IN olden times there was a man named Offerus, of such immense size and strength that men looked upon him almost as a giant; but they loved him greatly for his kindness and good nature. Offerus determined to employ himself in serving others, and while he was still very young he set forth on a journey to find the most mighty prince the world contained, to whom he might offer himself. He was directed to the Court of a powerful king, who rejoiced in possessing a servant of such enormous size and strength; and Offerus was well content, until one day he saw his royal master, at the mention of the name of the devil, make the sign of the Cross in evident alarm.

"What is that for?" asked Offerus.

"Because I fear the devil," replied the king.

"Then if you fear him, he is more powerful than you, and I will serve you no more," said Offerus. "I have resolved to give my strength to him who is mightiest; so I must take the devil for my master," and with that he left the Court.

After having travelled far, Offerus came upon a large company of horsemen, whose chief was black, and who spoke to him, asking what he sought.

" Oh, I am seeking the devil. I wish to serve him."

" I am he. If you wish to belong to my servants, I will receive you. Follow me." And thus Offerus was enrolled amongst the servants of Satan.

It happened that in one of their journeys the troop came to a large Cross standing at the corner of a road. The devil ordered them to retreat.

" What is that for ? " said Offerus.

" Because I fear the image of Christ."

" Then you are not so mighty as He ; so I will serve this Christ." And Offerus passed alone before the Cross, and continued his journey.

After awhile he met a holy hermit, of whom he inquired where he should find Christ.

" Everywhere," was the answer.

" I don't understand *that*," said Offerus ;
" but if such is the truth, can a strong man
like myself be of use to Him ? "

" You can serve Him by prayer, by fast-
ing, by vigils, my son," replied the holy man.
But a shadow passed across the face of
Offerus.

" Is there no other way in which to please
Him ? " he asked.

The hermit took him to the edge of a
torrent, which came down from the mountains, and said: " The poor pilgrims who wish
to cross this stream get wet, and are almost
borne away by its force sometimes. Stay
here, and bear across all those who come to
the bank; and if you do this simple service
for the love of Christ, He will one day ac-
knowledge you among His followers."

The plan pleased Offerus, and he began
to build a little cabin, in which he dwelt by

the water's edge, and by day and by night he carried across the torrent any pilgrim who asked his help.

One night, when he was sleeping, Offerus heard a childish voice calling him by his name three times. It was a dark night, and the stream was very deep and strong; but the great powerful man had no fear, and taking the little child who had called to him upon his shoulders, he stepped into the water.

When he reached the middle of the stream the torrent was unusually strong, and as he struggled through it with a difficulty he had never felt before, it seemed as if the child he carried became as heavy as a leaden weight. The thunder rolled overhead, lightning gleamed upon the water, and Offerus felt as it his burden increased every moment.

"How is it, little child, that you appear so heavy?" he said at last. "It seems as if I was carrying the world itself."

"Not only the world, but He who made it," said the little silvery voice. "I am Christ, thy Maker, thy God, thy Master. In return for the service thou hast offered Me, I baptize thee, in the Name of the Father, of the Son, and of the Holy Ghost; and name thee 'Christopher,' the bearer of Christ."

They gained the shore, and a sweetness filled the soul of the newly-made Christian. He fell prostrate in adoration before the Divine Child, Who thus addressed him:

"Rise, Christopher, and fix thy staff in the earth. To-morrow it shall bloom with white and fragrant roses, as a token that Christ has been thy burden this night," and

then the Holy Child disappeared amidst a
bright and glowing flame

The sun's earliest ray fell upon Christopher, still kneeling in silent adoration as he
had knelt before his Lord and Master, and
by his side was the staff, which had been dry
and withered, now covered with fragrant
roses such as once bloomed in Eden.

LEGEND OF THE MONK'S VISION.

A MONK was praying in his lonely cell, praying for greater self-denial, for strength in temptation, for pardon for the many sins of his life. Suddenly, as if with a flash of lightning, the little 'cell was illuminated by a brilliant splendour resting on its roof, its floor, its narrow walls, and the lonely monk saw before him a vision of his Saviour—not bleeding and dying, but standing there with a sweet face of love and gentleness in the midst of the radiant golden light.

With hands crossed upon his breast the monk bowed to the earth in wonder and adoration. "Oh, my Lord," he murmured, "who am I that Thou, the glorious God, should show Thyself to me? who am I that Thou shouldst come from heaven to visit my poor cell?" He was kneeling there in a rapture of love and wonder when the convent bell pealed loudly through cell and cloister. It was noon—the hour when there came every day, amidst the snows of the winter or the summer heat, a crowd of beggars to the convent door—the poor, the blind, the lame—to receive the food which the good monks supplied to them.

He who was wrapt in ecstasy before the vision of God was the monk whose duty it was to wait on them at the summons of the bell·

Now he hesitated—might he not stay? How could he leave that heavenly guest for a crowd of beggars at the gate? If he went, this glorious·vision would be gone before he could return, and he might never see it more. But while he lingered, a voice spoke to him in soft, clear tones: "My son," it said, "do thou thy daily duty; leave the rest to Me." The monk started to his feet —one lingering, longing look he gave to the blessed vision, then he quitted his cell and hastened to the gate, where the poor were clustering, eager and expectant. Long, very long the duty seemed that day; yet as he ministered to them the monk heard inwardly a voice which said, "Whatsoever thou dost to the least and lowest, thou art really doing unto Me."

At last the task was ended; every suppliant had been relieved, and the monk retraced his steps to his cell, musing as he went of the sweet face of the heavenly guest he had left there, who, alas! would be gone. But as he lifted the latch he saw the same marvellous golden splendour gilding the wall, the floor, the ceiling—there was the vision, still remaining as it had been when he left it in obedience to the summons of the bell; and as once more the monk bowed down before his Lord, with his heart filled with grateful love, the voice spoke again to him, saying: "My son, if thou hadst stayed, if thou hadst left undone thy daily duty, I must have fled."

LEGEND OF
THE ROSE OF HILDESHEIM.

T was a wintry day, the wind keen and the ground covered with snow, when Louis, the son of Charlemagne, Emperor of Germany, went out to hunt, attended by a numerous suite. Suddenly the prince found that he had lost a little silver cross, which was most precious to him, and which contained several holy relics; he always carried it about him, and his distress at missing it was very great.

He immediately ordered his attendants to
search in all directions for this sacred treasure, whilst he fervently implored God's
assistance, vowing that, if the cross was
discovered, he would build a church upon
the spot where it had fallen, in token of
his gratitude and joy.

The servants of Louis were full of confidence in the power of Heaven, and went
bravely into the thick masses of snow in the
forest to make their search, and soon they
observed a rose-tree in full bloom, from
which came a most sweet fragrance. They
advanced nearer, and then saw that in one
bud a small silver cross was raised like a
little altar amidst the snowy leaves, round
which shone a strangely dazzling light, and
they fell on their knees as they recognised
the prince's treasure, which was thus
miraculously restored in answer to prayer;

6 *

and, after thanking God for His goodness, they carried it reverently to their master.

The prince rejoiced greatly, and lost no time in erecting upon the spot a church, which should remain as a memorial of the power of the Almighty; and there, by the altar where the Divine Sacrifice is offered up, the spreading branches and pure white flowers of the rose-tree surround the tabernacle where the Lord is dwelling. Many hundred times the snow has fallen upon the forest, which has now disappeared and given place to the town of Hildesheim. The cathedral built by the pious Louis has stood for ages, and has even been attacked by fire; but the rose-tree has been miraculously preserved up to the present time as a sweet silent teacher of God's glory, and His goodness to those who turn to Him for help with faith and love.

LEGEND OF
THE CHILD OF MARY.

LONG, long ago, when the faith was pure and strong throughout England, a little girl tended her sheep in the green meadows and amongst the shadows of a wood. She was poor and ignorant; but God had taught her to pray, and had given her a yearning tender love for His Blessed Mother.

Her great longing was to visit some of the shrines of Mary. She had heard of these

from people who had talked with her; and
once a pilgrim, passing through that village,
had told the orphan girl of the little house
in which the Holy Family had lived on
earth — of its bands of pilgrims and the
costly gifts they made, of the waxen lights
and brilliant jewels round the golden shrine.
Then the little girl confided her trouble to
the pilgrim — that she could not see that
Holy Mother; that she could not even linger
in the old church in the valley, because it
was so far away; and the old man, as he
listened, smiled upon her and gave her an
image of the Blessed Virgin and Child.

"See, my daughter," he said, "I will fix
this for you in the trunk of this old tree.
This must be your shrine, and here you can
pray to your Holy Mother."

The little maiden was delighted, and it became her daily care to deck the image gaily.

True, she had no offerings of gold and gems; but she found the fairest flowers of the meadows, and briar roses of pure pale tint from the hedgerows, to twine around the humble shrine of her Queen; and even in winter she could make it wreaths of evergreen and holly.

This girl had neither parents or friends, and so she made a little humble cot under the spreading branches of the old oak; and here she dwelt, in poverty and want, unthought-of, uncared-for, but by God.

At length the priest from the distant village was summoned to the dwelling of the shepherd maiden, for the people found her ill and near her death. But when he reached the door he paused in silent wonder, for a lady stood by the lonely bedside, fair, majestic, with a band of costly gems round her forehead and a blue mantle covering her figure. With the gentle care of a mother she bent over the girl, wiping the dew of death from her forehead; pressing her lips on the cold thin cheek; speaking to her in words whose sweet tone the priest had never heard or imagined before.

"See, my child," said this lovely visitor, "the priest is here, bringing thy Jesus to thee. He will bear thee safely home."

Then the priest entered the hut. Trembling and on his knees he heard the last confession of the dying girl, and the lady raised her in her arms, while sweet strains of angel music filled the humble dwelling, because the Lord of Heaven had entered there. He has come to His suffering child, He rests in her heart, and the angel music sinks into faint sighing whispers. One glance of unspeakable love, of unimaginable longing, and the spirit of the shepherd-girl has fled.

The good priest is kneeling there all alone now, the radiant queenly form is no longer by the bedside, and yet the angel voices are singing, and yet a sweet fragrance lingers round the straw pallet. Then a soft voice whispered : "Tell this vision which you have seen. Tell it, that men's hearts may be moved to love. Say that none who call upon Mary shall die unaided. Say that she is a mother who will be always with her children in their need." So the good Father told his story for many a mile round; and the faith and love of the people caused them to build a little chapel on the consecrated spot, within which, for many a year, an oak tree might be seen with an image of Our Lady in its hollow trunk, wreathed with flowers and green leaves.

LEGEND OF
S. FRANCIS AND THE WOLF.

HERE was great fear in Gubbio. The men were afraid and troubled, and mothers clasped their little ones to their breasts in dismay, because of the terrible Wolf, who lurked in the forest on the hillside, which no hunter had yet been able to destroy. Many an unguarded flock of sheep had been attacked, many a little cradle had been left empty and blood-stained; and at length the townsmen met together in the market-place, to consult as to how they could capture the creature who was robbing them thus.

As they stood conversing with heavy hearts and anxious faces, the holy Francis joined them, in his hood and habit of brown, and they told him their grief.

"My children," he answered, "our Lord will send relief. He never refuses the petitions which are made to Him. Come with me to yonder mountain."

It was a long procession: the old, bowed down with infirmity; young men and maidens from the vineyards, little children laughing from their play; and so they reached the mountain, where S. Francis stood still, and called the Wolf to appear. Ah! why is it that the savage beast came down the mountain so peacefully on towards Francis, and then, gazing at him, stood still? Children shrank back with timid cries, women shuddered and turned pale; but all gazed upon the Saint with wonder.

"My brother Wolf," said he in a low and gentle voice, "thou little knowest the havoc thou hast made here. Thou hast devoured the young children, and filled the mothers' hearts with pain, thou hast brought loss and desolation into many a home; and yet, in all this, I cannot blame thee, for thou hast only followed the nature given thee by God. But now I must bid thee do the people of Gubbio no further harm. Thou must leave them to dwell in peace; while, on their part, they promise to give thee food."

Then Francis turned to one of the crowd and bade him bring some corn and brown bread, and as the Wolf eat it from the

Saint's hand a murmur of thanksgiving was heard from every one.

"Good brother Wolf, we will now part," said holy Francis. "As long as the men of Gubbio are faithful to their promise, thou, too, must hold to thine. Therefore, in token of this agreement, I bid thee place thy paw in my hand."

Wonderful power given by God to the pure in heart! a power to overcome even the savage nature of the animal. Slowly and gently it raises its paw, and lays it in the hand of the Saint.

From that day, regularly at noon, the Wolf came to that spot for his food; and when, at last, it was left untouched, and they knew the creature had gone from the forest, the people mourned after it as if they had lost a friend.

To this day mothers tell their children

the wondrous story of the Wolf upon that hill-side, and the people of Gubbio pray that the blessed Saint, who helped them in their distress, will now, and always, keep misfortune from their town.

LEGEND OF THE
SHRINE OF S. GEORGENBERG.

IN former times there was a young nobleman, who, having been enlightened by God to know the emptiness of all earthly joy and honour, resolved to forsake home, and friends, and riches, and live in the wilderness, alone with his Creator.

He travelled far, until he had left behind the green and pleasant valleys of his native land, and reached a wild solitude, where he cut out of the rock a little cave to shelter him, and there dwelt and prayed. Time passed, and he felt a great desire to visit the shrines of the Saints; so he took his staff in hand and went on pilgrimage, and after a year's absence he returned to his solitude, with a greater love for God in his heart and a still more fervent desire to serve Him perfectly.

He had brought back with him from Rome a beautiful picture of Christ's sweet mother, and with his own hands he wrought a little sanctuary to contain it; and from far and near the peasants came to venerate the image of Mary.

It chanced one day that a young nobleman had gone hunting the chamois among those rocky heights, and seeing many peasants toiling up a steep ascent he took the same path, and there, in the rocky cell, he found in the hermit his own elder brother, who had given up all for God. The young man was overjoyed with this unlooked-for meeting, and, in his happiness, made a vow, to build a chapel on the spot, in which pilgrims might kneel and pray.

No sooner was his project known, than all the people of the surrounding valleys, both lords and peasants, begged to be allowed to assist in his pious work, and it was commenced immediately. But, strange to say, it seemed as if God's blessing did not rest upon their labours. Nothing prospered; there were constant accidents, and the men were always hurting themselves with their tools; and, more surprising still, every day two snow-white doves flew down from heaven, and picking up every chip and shaving upon which blood from the injured men's wounds had fallen, carried them in their beaks and flew away.

7

At length the pious hermit, whose name was Reinhold, resolved that he would follow the doves, and see what they were doing; and when, after some search, he discovered their hiding-place, there lay before him a tiny, but perfect, model of a chapel, neatly fashioned from the chips which the birds had carried away. This servant of God recognised in this matter the Divine Will that he should remove from the spot where he had dwelt so happily for seven years, and, accepting the sacrifice, he begged his brother to build a chapel in the place which the doves had chosen for their resting-place.

His request was granted, and the little sanctuary was soon erected, and placed under the especial protection of S. George; and multitudes flocked there to pray, who had heard of the piety of Reinhold and of

his wonderful chapel.   Then many youths
of high rank became so attracted by the
holy example of the hermit, that they would
not leave him, and, in their turn, built little
cells and huts close by, where they devoted
themselves to a life of prayer and penance ;
and thus, in later years, a community of
holy monks was established, who followed
the rule of S. Benedict and kept alive the
faith in that land.

LEGEND OF S. URSULA.

A CERTAIN King and Queen, who dwelt in Brittany, had one only daughter, whom they named Ursula, and trained her in the fear and love of God. The maiden grew up beautiful and learned; but, far better than all, she was full of virtue and piety, and had dedicated herself to Christ for ever.

Not far from Brittany, on the other side of the great ocean, there was a country called England, whose people were still in the darkness of paganism, and the King of this land had an only son, who, having heard of Ursula, desired to marry her.

When messengers came to ask the King of Brittany for his daughter he was very much troubled, because he feared to refuse the request of the young Prince; and yet he dared not consent, for he knew that Ursula had pledged herself to be the Spouse of Christ. So he delayed his answer, and entertained the ambassadors very sumptuously, while he prayed God to deliver him from his great perplexity.

He was sitting apart, when his daughter came to him and asked the cause of his gloom; and, upon being told what had occurred, she smiled, and said: "Be not afraid, my father, for if it pleases you I will myself answer these messengers of the great King.

Next day Ursula, with much grace and modesty, went into the presence of the strangers, and having thanked them, as the representatives of the King, for the honour shown her, she said that she would promise to look on his son as her brother and bride-groom, and never to listen to another. But, first, she had three requests to make : one, that he would give her ten noble maidens for her ladies and companions, and to each of these and to herself a thousand virgins to wait upon them ; the second, that the Prince should give her three years to remain unmarried, with the permission to visit the holy shrines of the Saints in company with her attendants. The third demand was, that the Prince, and all his courtiers should be baptized Christians.

The ambassadors returned to their own country, with such accounts of the beauty and dignity of the Princess that the King of England thought no conditions too hard by which his son should gain this lovely bride; so he was at once baptized, with his courtiers, and sent commands to all his dukes and barons, desiring them to find for him the required number of pure and spotless maidens to wait upon the Princess Ursula, who was to wed his heir, the young Prince. The noble virgins came from all parts, and were welcomed gladly by Ursula; and so much wonder was caused in all the countries round about by the assembly, that people gathered together to view them.

Then all the young maidens were brought to Brittany. Ursula desired them to meet her in a meadow near the city, and there she spoke to them with so much earnestness of the purity and beauty of a life wholly consecrated to God, that they promised to follow wherever she should lead them; and many, who had not been baptized, received that holy Sacrament immediately.

Then Ursula wrote to the Prince, saying, that, having performed the engagement, he had her leave to wait upon her as a true knight. So he came at once to her father's Court to visit her, whereupon she said,—

"My gracious consort, it has been made known to me in a vision that I and my maidens must go to visit the holy city of Rome; and in the meantime do thou remain here to console and assist my father; and if aught happens otherwise to me, this kingdom shall be your own."

So Ursula, with her multitude of lovely virgins, embarked on board ships prepared for them, many holy prelates going in their company. There were no seamen in the vessels, for the good providence of God was their guide, and took them northward, instead of south, to the mouth of the Rhine. After proceeding some distance up the river, they landed and crossed the snowy Alps, with six angels for their guides, who went before to clear the path from obstacles, and to provide them tents in which to repose at night. Thus they journeyed to the holy city.

The Bishop of Rome then was Siricius, and hearing of the approach of these eleven thousand maidens, he was somewhat troubled, not knowing what it could mean; but he gathered together his clergy, and went out to meet them, and, giving them his blessing, commanded that they should be honourably lodged.

Meanwhile the affianced spouse of Ursula had journeyed to Rome by another way, in the hope of getting tidings of his bride;

and there he learned to aspire only to the
martyr's crown, and look to rejoicing with
Ursula in heaven alone.

Having visited the shrines of S. Peter
and S. Paul, the time had come for the
maidens to return to their own country,
and Siricius accompanied them as far as
the shore of the river where they should
embark. But on their arrival at the city
of Cologne, they found it full of barbarians,
who rushed to destroy the holy company,
and one of the first who fell was the young
Prince of England; then the holy Bishop
and several prelates sank upon the earth
or perished in the stream. Seeing the
danger of her friends, Ursula passed among
them, encouraging them to meet death
without fear, and by hundreds and thousands they perished, meekly resigned to
the Will of God. The plain was strewn

with martyred bodies; the river ran red
with blood; but the barbarians feared
to strike down Ursula; so they carried
her to their prince, who declared he would
make her his queen, the richest queen in
all Germany.

But Ursula defied him, saying,—

"Dost thou think I desire to live, when
my innocent sisters have died by the
sword? I scorn thee and him whom thou
servest, and I will never become thy
queen."

When the pagan heard these words he
was enraged, and bending his bow, pierced
her breast with three arrows, so that her
spirit ascended to heaven with her glorious
band of virgin-martyrs, where they stand
ever in the presence of their Divine Spouse,
blessing and praising Him.

LEGEND OF THE MOSS ROSE.

T was evening, as the Saviour took His way through the shady forest with pallid brow and aching head and feet, weary with the burning sand and sun of the desert. Now he felt the soft moss beneath His tread.

"What wondrous love My Father hath shown in thee," cried the Saviour. "Blind and dull must be the eye which cannot see in thy meanness the power of God. Bear, then, thy fate, lowly little herb : even if men do not prize thee, thou art not despised by thy Maker.''

Hardly had Jesus spoken these words than there sprang from the bed of soft moss a lovely little rose. And from that hour, in every land, the beauteous flower of the moss rose is considered as being the type of meekness, in remembrance of the favour it received for soothing the pain of Christ, and kissing those weary feet which crushed it beneath them. So shall we, if our hearts are faithful when pain presses heavily upon them, find that the fair sweet roses of meekness and joy will follow in due time.

LEGEND OF S. NICHOLAS.

IN the city of Panthera, in Asia Minor, there dwelt a nobleman, who had three daughters. He had been very rich, but poverty overtook him; indeed, his need was so great that he could scarcely find bread for his children. The maidens wept continually in their distress; and the good S. Nicholas, who dwelt in that city, happening to know their unhappy state, went one night, when the father was sitting alone weeping, after his daughters were gone to rest, and, with a large handful of gold tied up in a piece of linen, stood upon the threshold of the dwelling. He was wondering how to give the money without making himself known, when the moon shone out from behind the clouds and disclosed to the Saint a window, which he had not before observed, and which was open; so he threw in the gold, and it fell at the feet of the father, who received it with great joy, and with it gave a marriage portion to his eldest daughter.

A second time S. Nicholas provided gold, and again threw it in at the window, and with it the nobleman married his second daughter; but he wished very much to know who it was that had come to his aid, and so he determined to watch. When the good Saint came for the third time, intending

to throw it in as before, the father was
watching, and seizing him by the skirt of
his robe, flung himself at his feet, saying:
" Oh, Nicholas, servant of God! why seek
to hide thyself and thy charity?" and he
kissed his feet and hands in gratitude. But
the Saint hastened away, after forcing the
nobleman to promise that he would tell no
one of the gift.   And many such benevolent
works did Nicholas perform in his native
city, for he looked upon his great riches
as the property of God, to whom he was
as the steward who must render an account
of all.

LEGEND OF
THE FLOWERY CROWNS.

IT was Saturday, and in honour of the Blessed Virgin, the little Dominica had made two crowns of the loveliest flowers she could find; and then, kneeling on the ground before the images of Jesus and Mary, she offered to them each one, and, in her simplicity, begged that they would come down from heaven and smell the sweet fragrance of the flowers which she had picked for them.

When she found that they did not come, she thought it was her own sins which kept them from her, or because she had not first given alms to one of Christ's poor; so she rose from her prayer and ran to the window to look for some beggar to whom she could offer money or food.

There, in a ragged dress, she saw a woman who carried in her arms a little child, which cried piteously and held out its hand for a coin; and Dominica noticed that in each tiny palm there was a wound that moved her pity still more.

"Wait; I will come to you," she cried, and quickly ran to another room to ask for food for the mother and baby. When she returned, Dominica saw that they had come inside the house.

"Ah, what will my mother say?" she cried. "Who opened the door for you?

It will go hard with me, if you are seen in here."

"Do not fear; no one has seen us," replied the mother; but Dominica scarcely heard her, she was gazing with wonder at the feet of the little child.

" Why, how is this," she said, " your child has wounds in his feet too, and yet he can walk ? Do they not hurt you ? " she added, stooping down to the boy. But he only smiled, for his bright eyes had caught sight of the flowery crowns, and he stretched out his hands to take them. The woman reached the flowers, smelt them, and passed them to her child, and then turned to Dominica, asking her why she had crowned those two images.

"Because of the love I feel for Jesus and His Mother," replied Dominica.

" And how much do you love them ? "

8 *

asked the woman, smiling sweetly on the little girl.

"As much as I can," answered she.

Then the mother, noticing how Dominica gazed at her and the child, asked her what she was looking at.

"I am looking at your little son," said the girl. "Is there not a sweet odour which comes from those wounds? What is the ointment which you put on them?"

"The ointment of charity," answered the mother.

"Please tell me where it is sold."

"It is to be gained," said the woman. "Faith, prayer, and good works will get this sweet ointment."

Then Dominica offered bread to the child, but he refused it.

"Ah, his food is love," said his mother.

The little boy now spoke, in a clear sweet voice.

"Tell me how much you love Jesus," he said to Dominica.

"Oh, I love Him so much, I can hardly tell you," she answered. "I love Him so that I think of nothing else by day or night; and I want to do everything which pleases Him."

At this the sweet scent of the wounds grew so strong that Dominica cried out, "How fragrant Paradise will be, if a little child on earth can smell so sweet!" but even as she spoke the scene changed, the countenance of the child shone with such a glory that the little girl fell on her knees before him. She knew then that they were heavenly visitors; and the child, Jesus, took from His Mother's lap the flowers, and scattering them over Dominica said,—

"These are the promise of that which I will give you hereafter."

Then the Divine Child and His Mother vanished from her sight, and Dominica followed them with her heart.

LEGEND OF THE JEWISH CHILD.

THERE was at Bourges, in the earlier ages of the Church, a school, to which children of rich or poor families, whether Christians or Jews, could be sent without distinction.

One of the Jewish boys, a lad of twelve years, was a general favourite with his companions, though he was neither rich nor clever. It was because of his gentle, happy disposition they loved him, and they would linger after school was over to play with him in the cool evening hours.

The Christian children often ran into the church, and would kneel before an image of the Blessed Virgin, offering her flowers; and if their lessons were very hard to learn they would go and beg her to help them.

The little Jew did as the rest, and though he had learnt nothing about the Blessed Mother of God, he prayed to her as earnestly as any of them, and felt quite sure that she heard what he asked from her.

Easter - time came, and numbers of the children were to receive the Holy Eucharist, and as the bright morning light streamed in through the eastern window upon their earnest faces and spotless dresses, the little Jew felt such a longing to be one of them that the tears rolled down his cheeks with grief because he was not with the rest.

" Why might he not go with them ? " he asked himself. " Surely that sweet lady to whom he took his flowers would not shut him out from the children who looked so happy ! He too would receive the ' Christian's food,' " as he had learned to call it; and so, without any doubt or fear, he knelt with the others, and the priest, who was a stranger, gave him the Holy Communion in his turn. Poor child ! he had done it innocently, and perhaps no Christian boy or girl felt greater joy or made more earnest thanksgiving than the little untaught Jew.

Mass was ended, the boy paid a visit to his favourite image, and went home ; but he had been away so much longer than usual that his father asked him where he had been.

The child told him at once he had been to the Christians' church, and he spoke of the beautiful image, and how he loved to visit it, and then he said that on that very morning he had received the "Christian's food," which had given him such joy.

The father was furious with anger; it would be a blot upon his name for ever if it was known that his son had entered a church belonging to the Christians. At that moment he was tending a blazing furnace, and, in his rage, he seized the child, and, with bitter curses, threw him into the midst of the flames.

Presently the mother came out to seek her child.

"Where is the boy?" she asked her husband, who, turning away, made her no answer, and the poor woman, thinking he must be lost, began to run to and fro, questioning her neighbours, and calling the child by name, entreating him to answer her. Still he was not found; every corner in the house was searched in vain. At last the mother fancied she heard a voice which sounded like her son's, and she stopped to listen.

It seemed to come from the furnace, and as the neighbours, who had gathered together, stood still, in terror and surprise, the child's father rushed forward and attempted to throw another huge faggot upon the flaming pile; but one of them held him back, whilst others hurried to extinguish the burning wood and charcoal, and there at last they found the boy. But to their amazement, and the grateful joy of the terrified mother, they found that there was not even a hair singed; his cheeks were fresh and cool and rosy, and he told them, in his own simple way, that " the good sweet Lady of the church had caught him in her arms as his father threw him in, and kept him wrapped in the folds of her white mantle, so that he had never felt the flames."

The end of the father is not known, but the mother and child were baptized in the Christian church where the little Jew had learnt his first simple trust in the Blessed Virgin.

LEGEND OF S. ANTHONY.

WHEN the town of Rimini was filled
with heretics, S. Anthony desired
to gather them into the Christian church,
and explain to them the truths of the
Sacred Scriptures. But when he found
that they refused to listen to him, the
Saint, inspired by God, went down to the
seashore, and exclaimed, "Fishes of the
ocean, listen. I will preach to you the
Word of God, which these people refuse
to hear."

At these words, fish of all sizes rose up before S. Anthony in numbers which never before had been seen in that part, and ranged themselves in order to hear him.

"Fishes, my little brothers," the Saint began, "you should, as far as possible, return thanks to Him Who created you. It is God Who placed you where you are; it is He Who has given you the refreshing waters in which you live; it is He Who has provided for you innumerable places of retreat, where you can safely hide from those Who would destroy you, and who secures to you your necessary food. On the day of your creation, this God imposed upon you the order to increase and multiply; afterwards, at the time of the Deluge, you alone, of all other creatures, were preserved from perishing. To you He gave the keeping, for three days and nights, of His prophet Jonas. When the Lord Jesus Christ was poor upon earth, He received from you the means of paying tribute-money to Cæsar; and it was you who were chosen as food for Christ before and after His resurrection. In remembering these blessings bestowed on you by God, I call on you to glorify and thank Him from Whom you have received them."

At these words the fish inclined their heads and opened their mouths, as if trying to express their gratitude to their Maker. S. Anthony, transported with joy at the sight, exclaimed,—

"Blessed be the Eternal Father that these fish have rendered Him the praise refused Him by these people!"

On hearing of this miracle all the town came to witness it, and were so touched with compunction that they threw themselves at the Saint's feet and entreated him to instruct them. Then S. Anthony addressed them with such power and earnestness that many were immediately converted to the Church; and, after giving his blessing to the fishes, he dismissed the people to their homes; but during the few days he remained in Rimini, the Saint did a great and lasting work in the souls of all who heard him.

LEGEND OF
THE CHRISTMAS ROSE.

IT was near the holy time of Christmas, and the snow, which had been falling for many days, lay thickly upon the ground. In a small cottage a little child was crying with cold and hunger, for there was no fire upon the hearth, no food in the cupboard, and it was left alone while its mother went to the wood near by to gather faggots.

Poor little thing! it gazed out sadly upon the trees, all covered with snow, and as the

9

tears ran down its thin pale cheeks it cried, "Oh, when will the flowers come again— when will the warm sun shine? I wish there was a land where it was always summer, and where the roses bloom for ever."

The lonely child was startled by a voice which answered, "I will bring thee sunshine and give thee flowers too, if thou wilt play with me," and there, by the cottage door, stood a lovely little boy with a rosebud in his hand and a smile upon his face, and clothed in a white and sparkling robe.

"See! I have brought you summer-flowers," he said, in a sweet low voice, and the little one who listened saw that wherever he put his feet fresh blossoms sprang up in the path; and in his gladness he felt the cold no more, but drew his wonderful visitor inside the poor cottage.

For a long while they played together, and the stranger told of his own bright home so far away.

"But I must return there," the lovely little boy added; "I cannot stay with you; but I will leave you this sweet rosebud, and when it opens into flower I will come and take you home with me;" and then he disappeared, while the widow's child gazed at the spot where he had been standing with a longing look upon his little face. It grew dark, but the child was not unhappy: all his sorrow, and cold, and hunger had been forgotten, and he only wanted his mother to make haste that he might tell his wondrous tale.

When the widow came, and looked at the happy eager face of her little one, her heart was pierced with sorrow, for she knew it had been the Holy Child who had come to

9*

her poor home, and that very, very soon He would take her boy to heaven.

The Christmas-time had come, still the white snow lay thickly on the ground; but the wonderful rosebud had opened into flower and its rich fragrance filled the room. And there, on his tiny bed, lay the little boy, as cold as marble, with his blue eyes for ever closed, while his mother knelt by his side weeping, and wringing her hands, and moaning bitterly. But a sweet voice spoke to her, and as she strove to hush her sobs to listen it said :

"Why should you weep? Is not this earth a cold and dreary place? Is not your child happier and safer in My Father's house? Ah, poor weeping mother! you should rejoice, for your son is with Me here. Look up, and see his robes of dazzling white, radiant with the glory of heaven."

The widow raised her eyes, all dimmed with tears as they were; but no mortal ever knew what rapturous vision met her gaze, for, as she clasped her hands in an ecstasy of joy and love, her heart broke under its weight of gladness, and she too had reached the land where the sun shines always and where the roses never die.

LEGEND OF
SIR RODOLPH OF HAPSBURGH.

SIR RODOLPH of Hapsburgh rode at the head of his band of hunters, his bugle ringing out clear and sharply in the frosty air, causing the wild deer to bound over the rocky heights and hide themselves in the snowy Alpine forests. He was a brave young knight, as gay and glad as a child when engaged in the mountain chase, yet wise in council and earnest and reverent in prayer. There was not a stain upon his name ; his sword had never given a needless wound, though it had fought for many a one who was oppressed. Swiftly he rode, so swiftly that all his train were left behind, excepting one young page, and Sir Rodolph raised his bugle once more with a merry shout to call the loiterers onward.

But a soft silvery sound was borne upwards upon the frosty air, a sound which caused the knight to dismount in haste and kneel humbly on the ground with uncovered head. The lord of the mountains is bowing before the Lord of heaven and earth, Who is borne by an aged priest to the plains below, in the Blessed Sacrament which shall comfort and help the soul of one near death.

The priest paused beside the count, who whispered in low accents,—

" My reverend Father, for the dear sake
of Him whom thou dost bear upon thy
breast, grant me one request. Take my
steed for His service, and permit my page
and me to follow Him."

" Nay, Sir Knight," replied the old priest,
" how can this be, for already I can discern
thy train of huntsmen advancing to follow
thee in the chase ? "

"Father, to-day my men must hunt
alone, for, in truth, it would be a foul
disgrace if I rode on while thou on foot
should bear my Lord and King.   God
forbid that I should not follow Him who
died upon the Cross for me."

The priest mounted the noble steed,
while at his side, rein in hand, Sir
Rodolph walked with bent head and reverent step.   They went their way down
the rocky path to the plain below.   The

dying man received the Body and Blood of Christ, and then the little company ascended the hill once more.

As they enter the narrow mountain pass, the aged priest would restore the steed, but the Knight checks him.

" Nay, Father, I cannot mount again the charger which has borne my Lord; he has been a faithful friend to me, may he be the same to thee in thy journeyings. Farewell, my Father, yonder pathway will take thee quickly homeward; and I beg thee to remember my poor soul in thy prayers at Holy Mass."

The priest raised his hand in blessing upon the noble Knight, and then, gazing earnestly into his face, added,—

" When nine years have passed away, the Master whom thou lovest, and Who loveth thee, will reward the service thou hast rendered Him to-day."

The years rolled by: that brave young chief of Hapsburgh had grown into a stalwart knight, nor had he disappointed the promise of his early years, for he was first in name and rank among all Christian peers; and now the throne of that land was vacant, and serfs and nobles with one accord bent low before Sir Rodolph and chose him as their king.

The Count remembered then the words of the aged priest: " God will reward thy loyal service of to day when nine years have passed;" so he took his crown as the gift of his Creator, and ruled his subjects wisely and well, so that he might win the higher reward of an unfading crown in heaven.

LEGEND OF
THE FRIAR'S WARNING.

THERE was in olden times in Naples a convent of the Dominican Order, where the rule was but carelessly observed, and in which a spirit of pride and self-indulgence was creeping in among those who had promised themselves to the service of God. It was, however, the purpose of the Almighty to bring this community to a state of perfection, and thus a vision was granted them, which roused them to a spirit of greater fervour.   One day when the brother whose duty was the care of the refectory went to make ready for dinner, he beheld, to his surprise, a number of religious sitting on the benches, perfectly motionless, but there was something so terrifying in their stillness that his very flesh seemed to creep with fear as he gazed on them.

Then running to the Prior, the brother told what he had seen, explaining that these stangers who were in the refectory gave him such awful sensations of fear that he suspected they must be demons from hell.

The Prior was alarmed, and, after a moment's thought, he called the community together, and bidding them follow him to the church, he took out the Blessed Sacrament, that It might be carried in solemn procession to the refectory. He entered, followed by the brethren. Yes, it was indeed true, there sat the strange friars ; but as the Prior advanced, bearing our Divine Lord in his hands, they rose and prostrated their forms to the ground, and again seated themselves as silently as before.

Then said the Prior, " In the Name of God, Who is here present, tell me who you are, and from whence you come, and what you desire."

The strange company immediately threw back their hoods and displayed countenances blackened as if by fire ; then they opened their habits, and the red flames were seen consuming their very bodies, and one of them spoke these terrible words :

"We are all your brethren," said the voice : " behold us who were once priors, sub-priors, masters, and readers; and we are all eternally lost ! Lost for our contempt of poverty, for our neglect of rule, for our pride, our slothful-

ness, our self-indulgence; and we have come
here to warn you, lest, by like sins, you come
into like condemnation."

Striking a blow upon the table the strange
company disappeared. But their visit of
warning was not thrown away, for it sank so
deeply into the hearts of the brethren that
they became models of piety and perfection.

LEGEND OF
THE ENTRANCE TO HEAVEN.

ACCORDING to an old, old story, there was a day when the Holy Apostle S. Peter paced along the golden streets of the Heavenly City with a look of pain upon his face, as if he was sorely troubled, and S. John, meeting him thus, inquired what ailed him.

"Hast thou not seen here the faces of many who seem scarcely fitted for so glorious a home?" replied S. Peter, sadly.

"Little has it cost them to enter here, and yet we know that heaven must be gained by many a battle bravely won, by many a struggle and pain and temptation conquered."

"But thou dost guard the keys of heaven?" said S. John.

"I do. But though such is my post, it is S. Joseph who causes me this distress. No matter how sinful his life may be, if in death a person cries to him in faith and love, he brings them here. How they enter I can scarcely tell, for they do not pass the gate at which I stand: but I see them here, and it perplexes me, and I must speak to our Divine Master, lest He may think me careless in my duty of guarding the entrance to the Heavenly City."

S. John smiled. "Thou art Peter, and the Lord Jesus loves thee well," he said;

"and yet I tell thee that if S. Joseph plead against thee, thy cause is lost."

The great Apostle bethought him then of the night upon which S. John had rested his head upon the Sacred Heart of Jesus when He was on earth. Surely the love of the Lord for John was as great as He would feel for His foster-father.

"Come with me," he said; "thou hast ever been called the Beloved Apostle; no fear but the Master will listen if thou art by my side."

Together they stood before Jesus, who had Mary and Joseph on either side of Him.

"What is it, Peter?" said the gentle Voice.

"I am troubled, dear Lord," replied the Apostle, raising his eyes to the Divine Face. "It seems to me scarce just to those who serve Thee well on earth, if so many who

10

spend their life in sin, gain heaven after all. And yet it is S. Joseph who does this. All who call to him when they have to die are sure of his protection, and he brings them here among Thy martyrs and Thy saints."

"O Peter! dost thou not yet know that when I pardon the greatest sinner he wins life eternal? No soul is brought to heaven by S. Joseph which has not first sought Me, and been cleansed by the Blood which flowed on Calvary for the salvation of the world."

"Lord, I know that those who die in Thy grace shall surely see Thee," replied S. Peter. "I know that thus the dying thief found an entrance here, and many, many more. Yet, surely, it is not well for the Church on earth that S. Joseph should so easily gain admittance for all who cry to him. How, then, will sinners believe in the punishment of sin, and the judgment, severe and just, which follows death ? "

" True, Peter," said the Master; " yet what can I refuse my father, who guarded My childhood on earth, who worked and suffered for Me when. I was a weak and helpless Babe ? "

The Apostle bowed his head, still but half convinced, and, seeing this, the sweetest smile illumined the face of the Saviour.

"Ah, Peter, Peter," He said, " thou wouldst have none here but My chosen few, the few who gain heaven by true and faithful service. Dearly I prize this service, justly I reward it; but know also that I give heaven for love, that I who suffered so much to save mankind will have here in glory every sinner who dies contrite; nor do I wish that one should be shut out, however guilty, however miserable, who has turned in his last

10 *

moments to Me, the lover of sinners. Does this mercy indeed displease thee ? Wouldst thou choose a company of thine own, and not admit those who cry, 'Jesus, Mary, Joseph,' as they pass from earth ? "

Then the Apostle bowed low at the feet of his Saviour and King,—

" Lord, Thou knowest best," he murmured; " Thy Will I love, and to that Will I bend."

LEGEND OF
S. MARY MAGDALEN.

AFTER the time when S. Mary Magdalen had gone to dwell in Provence, a Prince and his wife arrived in that country, for the purpose of sacrificing to the heathen gods; but the words of the Saint had so much power over them that they refrained from this idolatry. One day the Prince told her how much he desired to possess a son, and asked her if she could obtain this blessing for him from her God.

Then said Magdalen to him, "If thy prayer is granted, wilt thou believe?"

He answered, "Yes, I will then believe in your God."

Soon after this the Prince wished to hear the preaching of S. Peter at Jerusalem, so he resolved to sail there, and his wife desired to accompany him; but he would not agree to take her, because of the dangers of the sea. However, she insisted, and throwing herself at his feet succeeded in obtaining her desire; so they set sail. But no sooner had a day and night passed than there came on a terrible storm, in the midst of which a little child was born, and the mother immediately died. The unhappy Prince, seeing his wife dead, and the infant, without any one to nourish it, crying for food, wrung his hands in despair, not knowing what to do or where to turn.

The sailors were desirous to throw the dead body into the sea; but the Prince prevented them, and as they just then arrived at a rocky island, he went on shore there and laid the body of his wife upon the earth, and holding the infant in his arms cried to S. Mary Magdalen to help him, and at least to save the life of the child which she had obtained from heaven by her prayers. Then he placed the little one upon the bosom of its dead mother, and, covering them both with his cloak, he went on his way weeping very sorrowfully.

When the Prince and his servants came to Jerusalem, the great S. Peter showed him all the places where the Saviour had been, and also instructed him in the Christian faith; and after two years were gone he returned to his own country, and passing by the island where he had left his wife's body, he landed there to visit and weep over her lonely grave.

Wonderful to tell, his infant son had been preserved by the prayers and protection of the Saint, and was accustomed to run about the sea-shore, gathering shells and pebbles; but when the child perceived a stranger upon the island it was afraid, because it had never before seen a man during its recollection, so it ran and hid under the cloak which covered its dead mother.

The Prince and all who were with him were filled with surprise at the miracle which had been worked in preserving the child, but their astonishment was still greater when the mother stretched out her arms, opened her eyes, and awoke from her long sleep of death.

Together the joyful prince and his wife

offered up thanks to God, and returning to their own land were immediately baptized; and upon hearing of this proof of the power of the Almighty, and the protecting care of His Saints, all the people of that part became Christians.

LEGEND OF
THE POOR SHEPHERDESS.

FAR away from the dwellings of man, upon a mountain-side, there was a little chapel of our Blessed Lady, to which few worshippers resorted ; only one poor Shepherdess knelt often there, praying to her Holy Mother, while her flocks browsed close by. It grieved this maiden to see the image of Mary unadorned ; and one day, having gathered some of the few flowers which grew in that part, she twined them into a garland, and, climbing on the altar of the little chapel, placed it on the head of the carved figure and said, "Dear Mother, would that I could place a crown of gold and precious gems upon thy brow but as thou knowest I am poor, I beg thee to receive this crown of flowers in token of the love I bear thee."

Many a day she renewed this little act of homage, wishing that she could better prove her devotion to Mary. And so time passed, and the Shepherdess fell ill, and was brought to the point of death. It happened then that two religious were journeying that way, and, being fatigued and footsore, they sat down under a tree to rest, and one fell asleep, while the other remained awake; but to both of them a heavenly vision was granted. They saw a company of very beautiful ladies passing by, amongst whom there was one of surpassing grace and dignity; and one of the religious addressed her, saying,—

"Lady, who art thou? and wherefore dost thou pass by these rugged ways?"

"I am the Mother of God," she answered. "I am journeying with these holy virgin saints to a neighbouring cottage, that I may visit one of my most faithful children, a humble shepherdess, who, during her life, has not forgotten to visit me," and as she said this she disappeared.

Then the servants of God exclaimed together, "We also will go and see her." So they started, and easily found the cottage of the poor dying maiden, where she lay stretched upon a bed of straw.

They spoke to her, and she answered, "Good brothers, do not pity me. Ask our Lord rather that you may be permitted to behold the glorious company, who are assisting me, and then you will rejoice for me and give Him thanks."

The brothers knelt down, and then it was permitted them to see Mary most Holy by the side of the dying girl, holding in her hand a crown, while she sweetly consoled and encouraged her.

Then the virgin Saints began to sing, and at the sound of the wondrous harmony the happy soul of the young shepherdess left her body, and Mary, placing the crown upon her head, led her to Paradise.

LEGEND OF ZAMORA'S WEALTH.

AMORA was by birth a Spaniard, and early in life he left his home for Mexico, where he engaged in trade and amassed considerable wealth, so that after a few years he resolved to return to his own land, there to enjoy his riches among his kindred.

As he journeyed towards Seville a thought came into his head that he would make a trial of the truth of his friends' affection. So when his father came out to meet him, he put on the air of a poor man, and when they asked him of his success he answered in the tone of one deeply disappointed.

His father, however, received him with unchanged love; but his brothers behaved coldly and neglectfully, and seemed vexed that they should not reap the benefit of his money, on which they had counted.

For four days Zamora kept them in ignorance of the truth; upon the fifth he left the house, cast off his mean dress, and returned clad in a velvet doublet and with a gold chain and the ornaments usually worn by cavaliers of that time. No sooner had the news spread than the coldness of his friends was exchanged for the greatest courtesy: the house was thronged with visitors, and his brothers vied with each other in expressing their affection.

But Zamora had found out how valueless was this regard. "Am I not still Zamora," he exclaimed, "the poor fool who could not make a penny for himself, though in the midst of gold? Yesterday, it is true, my dress was of fustian, and to-day it is of velvet; yet *I* am not changed. It is not me whom you love, it is my riches. In my father only have I found a faithful and constant heart."

Then dividing his money between his father and the poor, Zamora resolved to leave Spain for ever. The lesson he had learned of the worthlessness of human affection made so deep an impression upon his heart that he retired into solitude, where he might be separated from all ties to this life. After a short time he took the habit in a Dominican monastery, living among the brethren as one whose heart was fixed upon God alone.

LEGEND OF
THE WAYSIDE BEGGARS.

IN ancient times there were two young brothers, both noble, rich, and comely to look on ; but while the elder was kind, pious, and charitable, the heart of the younger was selfish and revengeful.

The father of these youths died while they were infants, but they had the blessing of a gentle and holy mother, who prayed daily for grace to train her sons aright.

It happened that they had to take a long journey to visit one of their kinsmen, and the brothers started forth in high spirits, with well-filled purses, warm clothing, and fleet horses to carry them on their way.

They had not travelled far before they came upon a poor woman sitting near a wayside cross, who hid her face in her apron and sobbed most bitterly. Antonio, the elder brother, reined in his horse to ask her what distressed her, and she replied that she had just lost her only son, who had worked for her support, and she wept because she was cast upon the charity of strangers.

The youth was touched with compassion; but his brother, who waited a little way off, laughed scornfully.

"What! You are going to believe the first pitiful story told you by the roadside?

The woman is a beggar, and wants to cheat you of your money. Do not linger."

"Hush, hush," replied Antonio. "Do you not see that she is just the age of our own dear mother? In remembrance of her I cannot pass this poor creature by;" so stooping down he gave the beggar-woman his purse, saying, "There is all the help I can give you; may God the Father be your consolation."

The poor distressed beggar pressed the purse to her lips, and prayed that Heaven might bless her benefactor, and then the brothers went on their way.

It was not very long before the road brought them to a dreary forest, and there they saw a little half-naked child, singing sadly to himself a strange melancholy air, while he clapped his tiny hands together, trying to warm them; and his teeth chattered in his head.

Antonio's kind heart was moved, and he exclaimed, " See, brother, how cold this poor child is : how he must suffer in the piercing wind."

Then Pietro laughed bitterly. "I do not feel the cold," he said. "This is but a peasant boy, who, doubtless, is used to it."

But Antonio murmured, "For the sake of Jesus I must relieve him," and reining in his horse he called the child to him and, handing him his own warm cloak, bade him say every night an Ave in return for the gift.

The brothers rode onward, but Antonio suffered from the cutting wind until they got through the forest and the sun shone out a little to warm him.

Presently they entered a green meadow, where an aged man sat, with a wallet on his back, and his tattered clothing marked him for a wanderer and a beggar.

When he saw the young men riding by, he called to them in beseeching tones.

Pietro took no heed; but Antonio approached the beggar, saying kindly, "What is it, father?"

"See my shrivelled cheeks, my bent form, my white hair," said the aged man. "My feet will carry me no further; I must sit here and die, unless you will lend me your horse to carry me on my journey.

Pietro heard, and laughed scornfully. Antonio looked thoughtful for a moment, and then said, "I give you my horse, old man, for the sake of Christ, Who has loved the poor so well. Thank God, in whose Name I bestow him on you," and then he gently helped the beggar to mount, and stood watching him on his way until he had disappeared from sight.

"Fool!" cried Pietro, angrily; "are you

not ashamed of what you have done?
Money, cloak, horse—all gone to three
miserable beggars, and you are reduced to
this state of want. I shall not share my
purse with you or give you a lift upon
my horse; it is better you should feel the
consequences of your own stupidity," and
he rode on his way, leaving Antonio to
trudge wearily on foot.

Was he sad? Ah, no; his heart was light
and joyous, for he remembered the words
of Him Who said, "Inasmuch as ye did it
unto one of these, ye have done it unto
Me;" and as he walked along he prayed
to the Queen of Angels to protect and
help him during his journey.

Meanwhile Pietro advanced rapidly, and
came to a narrow path between two rocky
mountains, where no gleam of sunshine
entered, and where all was gloom. The

wind moaned drearily, and Pietro shuddered and looked round him affrighted. Ah! well might he tremble and shiver, for the form of the Evil One rose before him, black and gaunt, bidding him follow, and claiming him as his own possession. With a terrible shriek the youth fell fainting from his horse, and lay senseless in the pathway until some hours after, when Antonio reached the same spot, which for him had no terror, because his Blessed Mother was watching over him.

On perceiving the state of Pietro, the pious youth sank on his knees and prayed God to save his brother. As he spoke, a radiant light illumined the mountain-tops, and three glorious Angels appeared there, who looked down lovingly on Antonio.

"Fear not," said one, in tones of silvery sweetness. "The woman, the child, and the aged man whom thou didst help were none others than our Blessed Lady, her Divine Son, and the holy Saint Joseph. They have sent us to guard and help thee, and, for thy sake, to help and restore thy brother also."

Then the three angels spread their wings and soared above the pathway like three white doves, and Pietro rose up, and, with Antonio, followed the heavenly spirits until they had passed through the gloomy mountains; then the lovely messengers vanished amidst soft strains of music, while the brothers, looking around, saw both their steeds fastened to a tree in waiting for them. Mounting, they went their way— one humbled, contrite, and changed in heart; the other praising God and Mary Immaculate.

LEGEND OF THE NUN'S BEADS.

THERE was a very earnest and devout Nun, who had a great love for the Blessed Mother of God, and whose every spare moment was given to the recital of the rosary.

She was, however, so busily occupied in the service of the community, that it was often a difficult matter to complete her work and her prayers in the day, so that sometimes she had to rise in the night to fulfil some duty.   One night she was winnowing flour, and as she worked in solitude and silence the thought came into her mind that she might say her rosary at the same time. So she worked at her flour with one hand as she passed the beads through the other, and thus employed, the hours sped rapidly away.

At last, happening to cast her eyes on the table where her beads rested, she saw many lovely roses lying there. For every Ave she had said there was a white rose, for every Paternoster a red one; and yet, though the flowers were plainly to be seen, the humble Nun could scarcely believe such a wonderful thing could happen to her. So she went on with her prayers; but, watching, she saw that at each one which fell from her lips a fresh rose appeared on the table. She could not doubt any longer the favour which had been granted her, although she resolved to conceal it from her sisters, through humility.

But such was not God's Will, for He, Who loves to listen to every prayer which is offered through Mary Immaculate, caused the beads of this pious Nun to change into garlands of fragrant roses even when she prayed in public, so that thus all might see the reward of devotion to her whom He chose for His Mother.

LEGEND OF
CHARLES, KING OF SICILY.

WHEN Charles II. of Sicily and Count of Provence was taken prisoner, and confined at Barcelona, his confessor advised him to ask the intercession of S. Mary Magdalen, the special patroness of Provence, because it was in that region she passed the long period of her penitential life.

King Charles did what was recommended to him, and on the next night, which was the night of the feast of this great Saint, he was aroused from his sleep to see her standing by his side.

"I have heard your prayer," she said. "Arise, and follow me."

He rose, and S. Mary Magdalen led him and all his followers, who had been made prisoners, safe out of the fortress, and for a little while she still continued to walk on before them in silence, and they wondered very much where she was leading them to.

At last she turned and asked the King if he knew in what country he was. He replied, "Yes; we are just outside the walls of Barcelona."

"You are mistaken," said the Saint; "already you are six miles beyond the boundaries of Spain and Provence, and only one league from Narbonne."

Charles threw himself at her feet. "What shall I do," said he, "as a token of my gratitude for this night's deliverance ? "

S. Mary Magdalen smiled graciously upon him.

" I will tell you what you shall do," she answered. " Many long years ago, when war was raging in this province, my relics were moved to the church of S. Maximin by the faithful. There they still lie, and I bid you search for them. A vine grows there, and underneath it you will find my body, and by this token you may know it is truly mine—the skin is unchanged on the part where it touched our Lord's risen body. Two vessels also you will find, one filled with the hair which wiped His sacred feet, the other preserves the blood-stained earth which I gathered at the foot of the Cross on the day of His suffering there. Those precious relics never left me while I lived, and with me they were buried. I desire now that they are given into the keeping of the Friar Preachers, who are my brothers, seeing that I also, like them, was a preacher and an apostle," and with these words the Saint disappeared.

When day dawned, Charles of Sicily, Count of Provence, saw that he was indeed close to Narbonne, and, in remembrance of the miracle, he erected a cross over the spot and went to the church of S. Maximin to search for the holy relics.

There he found them, as the Saint had said; and when a monastery of the Dominican Order was erected, the relics were removed there with great pomp, and the King had ever after a deep devotion for the Saint who had come to his help in answer to the prayer he addressed to her when he was a prisoner.

LEGEND OF
THE MAIDEN'S VIGIL.

ONE Christmas Eve, long years ago, a maiden knelt in her little oratory, praying earnestly to Him Who once came into the world as an infant at Bethlehem, and while she thought of His sufferings in that poor cave, her heart was all on fire with love.

As she prayed, a bright light filled the room, and Mary appeared with the Divine Child, Whom she placed in the young girl's arms. Then the Lord, in softest tones, said to her: "How much dost thou love Me?"

She answered in the words of S. Peter: "Lord, Thou knowest that I love Thee."

"But how much?" asked the Infant Saviour.

"More than myself," murmured the maiden.

"And dost thou really love Me?" said the gentle voice again.

"Yes, yes, Lord," cried His little spouse; "I love Thee, and Thou knowest it, more than my heart and my life."

"How much more than thy heart?" inquired Jesus.

Then the maiden drooped her head. "I know not how to answer Thee, my dearest Lord," she said; "my heart itself should speak," and such was the force of her love, which could find no expression in words,

12

that her heart broke. Just a few moments she lay conscious, so as to tell those who found her on the floor of her oratory what had happened—then she was gone to hear the Christmas song of the angels in heaven.

LEGEND OF
THE HAWTHORN TREE.

IT was noon-tide, and the burning rays of the eastern sun came down fiercely upon the yellow sand of the desert over which S. Joseph with the Virgin Mother and her Child travelled on their way to the land of Egypt. Not a tree or bush was there to shelter them, and much did the travellers suffer from thirst and heat; yet they murmured not, but passed the time in whispered prayers.

Suddenly the ass stopped, and would not go forward. What was to be done? They were about mid-way in the desert, and no help could be obtained. No wonder that S. Joseph looked anxiously at the Blessed Virgin and her Divine Son.

But as they stood dismayed, the little Jesus stretched out His hand and smiled, and the travellers saw before them, but a few paces distant, a little stunted, withered bush which they had not noticed before; and the holy Mary alighted and spread her cloak there, so that the Holy Child might rest.

But in that moment, instead of a poor withered shrub, it was a blooming tree of hawthorn, full and shapely, covered with white and fragrant flowers; and beneath its shade sprang up green fresh grass, amidst which flowed a spring of water.

Reverently and devoutly did the good S. Joseph and the holy Mary thank God for His gifts, while white-robed angels came towards them bringing cooling fruits to relieve their thirst.

Then, the Infant Saviour said, " Mother, as this poor shrub did bloom for thee this day, so shall those souls bloom with virtue and grace who seek a shelter in thy heart. And in remembrance of this promise it is My Will that this bush shall flower always in the month which Christians yet unborn shall consecrate to thee, and angels shall carry its seeds throughout the earth that men may know its pure white blossoms and with them adorn thine image."

So the Blessed Virgin took up her cloak, on which the little Jesus had rested, and as they continued their way, the angels divided the branches of the tree which had been so blessed, carrying them to different parts of the earth, as the Divine Child had said, while they sang the praises of God and the purity and sweetness of His Blessed Mother.

LEGEND OF EINSIEDELN.

AMONG the rocky mountains of Switzerland the holy monk Meinrad built himself a little cell and a small chapel; in which he placed an image of the Virgin Mother, before which he had knelt many hours in prayer and received some miraculous favours.

It was a quiet peaceful retreat, but the enemy of souls sought to disturb the holy man by many assaults, as he has always sought to trouble the lovers of God. At times the whole forest seemed in flames around his cell, and terrible storms shook the pine-trees of that dense forest, yet Meinrad remained unmoved and unharmed, with prayer for his unfailing weapon.

A monk from a neighbouring monastery, who was permitted sometimes to visit him, drew near the cell of Meinrad one night and saw a brilliant light streaming from the little chapel.

Looking in he observed the pious and holy man kneeling upon the altar-step reciting the night Office, while a young and lovely child supported the book, reciting with Meinrad the alternate verses. The monk retired full of reverence and awe to tell his brethren that Meinrad was visited by angels.

For many years the holy hermit pursued his life of prayer, penance, and labour. The simple peasants sought his instruction, and even the wild animals of the forest and the birds of the air resorted to his humble and lonely cell.

At length two wicked men, who had pondered long over the devotion of Meinrad to his image of Mary, decided that it must contain some hidden treasure of great value, and they conceived the idea of killing him, so that the prize might be theirs.

They made their way to his cell, and as they passed through the forest the birds raised their voices as if to warn their friend of his danger; but God had already made known to Meinrad what was to happen, and, with a look of compassion, he addressed his would-be murderers,—

"I know what brings you here," he said; "but you shall receive my pardon and blessing before you slay me. When I am

dead put these two candles, one at the
head of my couch, the other at its foot,
and then fly quickly, lest you may be discovered."

The wretched men were not softened by
his words. They dashed out his brains, and
then searched for the hidden treasure which
they believed was there. But they sought
in vain, and, in their rage and disappoint-
ment, were leaving the place so hastily that
they forgot the request of Meinrad until
they beheld the candles lit, but by no
earthly hand.

Terrified at this strange and wonderful
occurrence, they hurried along the narrow
pathways of the forest, dreading to let their
bloodstained hands and clothes be seen;
but two crows who had often been fed by
the murdered Saint pursued them, flapping
their wings and pecking at them.

During that day a poor carpenter went to the cell of Meinrad, and there found him dead. When the news spread, some people remembered having seen two men hurrying along towards Zurich, and they pursued them there, believing that it was they who had committed the murder.

On reaching the town they found the two crows pecking at the window of a room in which the men had taken refuge, in spite of the efforts of the servant to drive them away; and when these birds were recognised as those who had frequented the cell of Meinrad, the murderers confessed their guilt, and gave themselves up to justice. They were executed in punishment for their crime, and at the moment of death the two crows still hovered above the scaffold.

After this the little cell and chapel of Einsiedeln were visited by many devout people, who came to pray before the image of the Blessed Virgin which Meinrad had prized so much ; and some years afterwards a magnificent abbey rose upon the spot, which had been consecrated by the life and death of the saint.

LEGEND OF S. GREGORY.

WHILE the holy S. Gregory was still a monk in the Monastery of S. Andrew, a beggar came to the gate asking alms. He was at once relieved, but he came again and again, until at last the charitable Saint had nothing left to bestow. This grieved him exceedingly, and he was thinking sorrowfully of his poverty when he suddenly remembered that he had still a silver porringer, which had been the gift of his mother, and accordingly he commanded that it should be bestowed upon this importunate beggar.

At a later period of his good life, when he had become pope, S. Gregory made it a practice to entertain twelve poor men every evening at his own table, in remembrance of the Twelve Apostles of Christ. One night, as he sat among his guests, he saw, to his amazement, thirteen there, instead of the twelve who had been invited; so he called his steward and said to him,—

"Did I not command thee to bring twelve to my table? Behold there are thirteen present!"

The steward looked amazed, and counted the guests over, but having done so he exclaimed,—

"Holy Father, there are surely only twelve!"

The holy S. Gregory said no more then, but when the meal was over he called the uninvited guest to him, and said, "Who art thou?"

Then the poor man replied, "I am that beggar whom thou didst relieve so often at the monastery gate; but my name is Wonderful, and through Me thou shalt obtain every favour thou desirest of God."

Then the Holy Father knew that his guest was none other than Jesus, his Divine Lord.

LEGEND OF
THE LITTLE NOVICES.

WHEN the Blessed Bernard filled the office of sacristan in the Convent of Santarem, the time which he had to spare from the service of the altar was given to the care and teaching of two children who were sent daily to the convent from their father's house near by. These boys were allowed to wear the habit of Dominican novices, as they were to be received into the community when they were old enough, and Bernard felt a great joy in training them, because he was sure their gentle goodness and innocence must make them very dear to his Divine Master.

The little boys were allowed to go into a small chapel at the side of the high altar, and they would spread out their books upon the steps, and study there happily and quietly, or eat their dinner, which they brought with them from home. This chapel was but seldom used for saying Mass, but on the altar there was an image of Mary with the Holy Child in her arms, and the little novices used to talk to the Divine Infant, as if He was a companion, with all the simplicity of their age.

"Dear Holy Child," said one of the boys one day, "how is it that you never move, as we do, never eat, but always stay in your Blessed Mother's arms We will give you

13

our dinner so gladly, if you will come down and eat with us."

It was God's Will to reward the faith and simplicity of the children by a wonderful miracle, for the carved form of the Divine Child took the appearance of life, and, coming down from its mother's arms, sat with the boys before the altar, and took some dinner with them.

This happened more than once, and that little chapel seemed to the young novices full of the joy of heaven, and they grew in such burning love to the Holy Jesus that they cared for nothing but His presence, and waited wearily for the happy hour when they hoped He might come to them.

Their parents saw that a great change had come over the children, and that they were never happy away from the convent; and, after questioning them closely, the little novices told their wonderful tale, but it was said to be only an idle foolish fancy, that such a thing was impossible, and they were reproved for thinking of it.

The Blessed Bernard heard what the little lads told him with very different feelings. He knew that to our Lord—Who loved little children so much that He took their form when He came into the world—nothing was impossible ; and when he felt quite satisfied that they had spoken truthfully, he bade them give thanks to God for His goodness. Then hearing them say, in their childish way, that they wondered the Holy Infant did not bring some food, too, for them to eat with Him, Bernard bade them ask their heavenly visitor, at His next coming, whether He would not invite them to dine with Him in His Father's house.

The boys were delighted with this injunc-

tion, and did not fail to repeat the words
of their master; at which the Child Jesus
smiled radiantly, and said, "Within three
days you shall indeed come with Me to My
Father's house," and the novices ran back
to tell Bernard of this gracious invitation.

Bernard looked lovingly on his pupils,
although there was a feeling of sadness in
his heart, for he knew what the message
meant; he knew the purity and innocence
of their young hearts, and was sure that
in some wonderful way God was going to
take them from the world before they had
been stained by sin.

It would cost the holy man a sorrowful
pang to give them up, for they had grown
very dear to him; and yet he rejoiced that
they had been chosen to be thus blessed.
Then a great longing filled his breast that
he, who was growing old in the spiritual

life, might pass away to his Lord, too, and he bade the children return and tell the Infant Jesus, that they who wore the habit of S. Dominic must keep the rules, and that, being novices, they might not go anywhere unless their master was with them.

"Then," said the Holy Child, "return to your master, and bid him prepare, for on Thursday I will receive him, with you, into My Father's house."

Bernard's heart was stirred with the deepest emotions of joy and love when he heard this welcome message, and he began to arrange everything, and to get ready for his death.

The day fixed was Ascension Day, and after obtaining permission, the Blessed Bernard celebrated the last Mass that morning, his little pupils acting as servers and receiving the Holy Communion from his hands;

and when the Mass was ended, he knelt
upon the altar-steps with a child on each
side of him, commending his soul to God.

About an hour afterwards some of the
brothers passing through the church saw
Bernard still kneeling there, vested as
for Mass, with the little novices in their
dress of servers at his side; but the three
were quite dead, and the soft smile upon
their faces showed that they had indeed
gone home with the Holy Child in the
very act of prayer. They were buried in
the chapel where their Lord had visited
them so often, and a picture was hung
above the altar, representing the little
novices seated upon the step, with the
Divine Infant between them.

LEGEND OF S. PATRICK AND THE TWO PRINCESSES.

TWO royal maidens were hastening in the early dawn of morning to bathe at the well of Clebach; but suddenly they stopped, for on the stone there sat S. Patrick grasping his crozier, and they knelt before him, not in fear, but in loving reverence.

Patrick rose and made the sacred sign three times, and then the maidens asked him why he came to the land of the king their father.

"I come from a greater Kingdom, the Kingdom of God," said the Saint. "There is rejoicing and gladness; there the poor and needy are welcomed by the love of the king; there is the fruit of immortal life, and a garden, in the midst of which sits One upon a golden throne, girded round with the rays of Seven Virtues, in which His holy ones are washed free from sin."

"Oh tell us Who is your God then," cried the sisters. "How can we find Him and love Him?"

Then the Saint told them of God the Father, Son, and Spirit, of the peace and joy which the pure and spotless might inherit, and of the Divine Spouse whose Brides they might be if they would. And when he told them of the sorrows of the King's Son, of the wounds in His Hands, and Feet, and Side, the tears ran down their faces.

"We will kiss those bleeding Feet," they cried. "We will renounce all that is sweet on earth for that wounded Heart. Shew us the way to His glorious palace."

"It is a rough way—narrow, thorny, steep," replied Patrick. "A way by which none can walk but those who have been cleansed in the waters of Baptism."

They knelt, and in the Name of the Blessed Trinity, he poured the stream upon their heads, and signed upon each forehead the Sacred Sign.

"But we would see the great King's Son," cried the newly made Christians. "We *must* see Him or die."

"They only see His face who have tasted of His Eucharistic Sacrifice and washed in the Bath of Death."

"Oh give to us that Sacrifice," and each bright head bent towards It: the blood fled from their warm cheeks, the young lives ebbed away, and, smiling in death, they breathed no more.

The king and the courtiers stood mutely by the dead maidens, for the rumour had spread; and dark-robed Druids and Bards drew near. But when S. Patrick raised the "Staff of Jesus," the stony-hearted were softened, for angels' voices were heard singing above them.

The Brides of Christ lay by the well of Clebach, and a green mound was raised above them; and that grave was given to the Saint, who built above it a church in remembrance of those who had been thus espoused to Heaven.

LEGEND OF THE HOLY WELL.

WHEN the Blessed S. Winifred was still but a child, she was given the desire to devote herself wholly to God's service, and to consecrate her virginity to her Heavenly Spouse.

But the enemy of souls put into the heart of Cradocus an impure love for Winifred, which occasioned him to visit her one Sunday, when her parents had gone to church before her, hoping to induce her to violate her promise to God.

Under the pretext of arranging her dress in a manner befitting the entertainment of the son of a king, the Saint escaped by a private door, and ran immediately towards the church to seek protection there.

The prince, impatient of her delay, sought her; and finding she had escaped, pursued her so eagerly that he overtook her on the descent of the hill, and in his fury drew his sword, with one blow separating her head from her body.

The head rolled down the hill to the church where the congregation were assembled before the altar, but their terror at the sight of this bloody object was changed into astonishment as they beheld a clear and rapid spring gushing out of the very spot of ground her head had first fallen on—a place which had, before her death, been known by the name of the Dry Valley.

The grief of the parents on witnessing this act of barbarity was intense, and the people with united voices called aloud for Heaven's vengeance upon the murderer, who stood wiping his bloody sword upon the grass, glorying in his detestable act.

The holy priest S. Beuno had been preparing to offer up the Adorable Sacrifice of the Mass, but inspired by God he left the altar, and taking the Blessed Martyr's head in his trembling hands, mounted the hill advancing towards Cradocus.

"Thou wicked man," he said. "Thou hast massacred a virgin as nobly born as thyself, and yet thou seemest not to repent of this horrible sacrilege. Therefore I beseech my Heavenly Lord that, for an example to others, He will be pleased to execute His judgments against thee for murdering His spouse, troubling His people, and sprinkling

His holy house with blood." At these words, it is said that Cradocus not only dropped dead, but the earth opened and gave his body a passage to the devil, whom he had served.

Still the people and the desolate parents deplored the untimely death of the holy virgin, and S. Beuno earnestly begged of God that as He had commanded Lazarus back to life, so for His greater honour and glory He would graciously raise up Winifred once more to His service on earth. Then joining the Martyr's head to the lifeless body, he covered it with his cloak and began the Holy Sacrifice.

After Mass was ended the good priest prayed fervently to God, and, to the joy of all the pious people who witnessed the miracle, the virgin arose like one just awakened from sleep, and with her hand wiped away the dust which had settled on her head when it rolled to the feet of S. Beuno. Her parents and others, looking at her neck, observed there a pure white circle no larger than a thread just where the separation had been made, which remained ever after as a mark of the affection of her Divine Spouse for suffering so courageously for His sake.

S. Winifred associated herself with other noble virgins, and spent a life of devotion in the service of God, Who was pleased to declare by signs and miracles the favour with which He regarded her.

The stones of the miraculous well are to this day stained with blood, to perpetuate the memory of that which she shed for Christ; and it was found that the moss growing there had a very sweet fragrance, as an emblem of her angelical virtues.

Multitudes of pilgrims still flock to the

spring and are healed by bathing in its
waters; asking through the intercession of
S. Winifred those temporal and spiritual
favours which shall promote their eternal
salvation and the holy service of Almighty
God.

LEGEND OF
S. JOHN THE EVANGELIST.

DURING the time that Christ's beloved Apostle S. John dwelt at Ephesus, he had a young man of great promise under his care and guidance, for whom he offered up many and constant prayers to Almighty God, while he sought to shield his pupil from all the temptations of the world. But the Apostle was obliged to go on a journey, and so he entrusted the youth to the care of a certain Bishop during his absence, bidding him watch over him as a son.

For a little while all went well, but afterwards this young man was tempted by evil influence, and at length was drawn so far from God and the path of virtue, that he became the chief among a band of robbers, who were the terror of the country round about.

When S. John returned to the city, his first act was to seek the Bishop, asking for the youth he had committed to his keeping.

The priest, with shame and sorrow for his want of watchfulness, cast down his eyes as he related what had happened, and the holy Apostle rent his garments and wept bitterly over the loss of one whom he had sought to train in the service of God.

But he could not let his former charge remain in sin without trying to reclaim him; and when they told him that he was hiding in the forest with a strong band of robbers,

and none could venture there with safety,
S. John only called for a horse and rode
with haste to the gloomy thicket where the
men were supposed to be concealed. Many
a bramble and thorn did he battle with in his
course, as the underwood grew darker and
thicker. Leading his horse by the bridle, he
threaded his way through the narrow foot-
tracks, parting the branches of the leafy
trees and forcing a way through the en-
tangling thicket, his thoughts all turning
lovingly to the one he sought, while he
prayed unceasingly for power from above
to win back that sin-stained soul to God.

At length he heard a footstep come crash-
ing through the briars and brambles, and in
another moment the captain of the robber
band—his old pupil—stood before him with
the fierce countenance of one resolved to
plunder the stranger who had ventured into

14 *

that solitude. One instant only did the man's eyes glisten with revenge, the next he had recognised his friend and master; and God's grace, poured into that long-closed heart—enlightening him to see all his sin and faithlessness—so filled him with remorse that he would have turned and fled to hide his misery and shame, had not S. John thrown his arm around the robber's neck and thus detained him.

Then, with tears fast flowing on those guilty hands, the holy Apostle besought him earnestly to repent and be reconciled to God. At length the robber yielded, and flinging down his weapons, humbly and penitently followed his master back to the city, where he ever afterwards led a life of holiness and deep contrition.

LEGEND OF THE ABBOT JOHN.

A LITTLE company of holy monks knelt humbly to receive the blessing of the Abbot of the monastery, where they had long dwelt happily, before taking their way through the pleasant English valley in search of some spot upon which they might found another house to the praise and glory of God. For their guide they had their Divine Master; for their comforter His Blessed Mother; while one

of the number—the pious John Kingston
—had been chosen for the head of the
monastery they should establish. They
carried with them some sacred relics, and
a copy of their holy Benedictine rule, and
commenced their journey in a spirit of
cheerfulness and courage, raising their
hearts in prayer to Heaven as they went
on their way.

When night came, the brothers rested
in a certain town; and, during his sleep, a
revelation was granted to the Abbot John.

It seemed to him that, as he passed
through the cloister at Byland, a lady of
marvellous beauty appeared before him,
holding by the hand a lovely little child,
who plucked a bough from a little tree which
was there, and then was lost to sight.

Then, in his dream, John went to the
outer gate, where his brethren awaited him,

and as they walked along he asked them if they knew where they were going; to which they answered that they did not.

They went on a little farther, and it appeared as if the thorns and brambles hedged them in so that they could see no path, neither could they discover the way by which they had come, so as to retrace their steps. To soothe their perplexity and distress they began to recite their Office and the Gospels, and when they had finished, the beautiful lady and her little son whom Abbot John had seen in the cloister, appeared once more.

Then he implored her to lead him and his brethren upon their road, begging her help for the love of those who served and honoured her in the monastery at Byland. The Lady, who was the Blessed Virgin herself, turned to the Holy Child Jesus and bade Him guide the monks on their way, and then she departed, while her Son held out the branch He had plucked in the cloister, saying, in a soft clear voice,

" Have confidence, and follow me."

Along rough hard ways the brethren passed, but they knew no weariness; and a number of little birds as white as snow fluttered round them, lighting on the bough and singing so sweetly that the monks were ravished with delight.

At length they reached a spot where the Divine Child planted His branch in the earth with the birds singing on it, saying as he did so,—

" Here will God soon be adored."

Then it seemed that the small weak bough grew in a moment to the size of a great tree, and bidding the brothers rest there, their Heavenly Guide vanished.

After this strange vision Abbot John slept little, for he was pondering in his heart what it could mean; but he felt a fresh confidence and peace as he rose to proceed on his journey in the early hours of the morning, when the light of the moon and stars still appeared in the sky; and, cheering his companions by the account of the favour he had received from Heaven, they presently arrived at the place to which the Blessed Virgin had directed them, and there an abbey was founded under her especial patronage, where she was loved and worshipped for long ages by the hearts of her faithful children.

LEGEND OF THE SNAKE.

IN olden times—those far-off times when the sweet Infant Jesus was dwelling in the world—a group of merry children played together on the grass while their mothers were busy with household duties, though listening as they worked to the glad laughter which rang upon their ears.

Suddenly a piercing scream was heard. The women stood motionless with fear,

then ran to the little ones. A terrible
sight met their eyes : a child lay pale and
motionless upon the greensward, with a
black snake coiled around his curly head,
whose venomous bite had poisoned the
young life, his small hands still grasping
the bright blossoms he was gathering for
a garland when the reptile had silently
and swiftly approached him in his un-
conscious happiness.

Bitterly his mother wept; so bitterly that
she did not hear the quiet step of Mary,
leading by the hand her Holy Child. A
smile played upon the rosy lips of Jesus
as He came to the side of the dead child;
and even as He advanced, the snake felt the
power of His presence, and unwound itself
from the fair little head.

"O reptile," cried the Saviour, "who
hath given thee power to slay this child?

For this deed of cruelty thou shalt die, that all may see the power of God, My Father."

In an instant the snake was dead, and the little child opened his eyes, and, smiling as his gaze met that of Jesus, he rose and knelt in gratitude at the feet of that Divine Saviour, Who should one day save from a more terrible doom the race of man, and whose voice and touch should give life and healing to those who lay dead in sin.

LEGEND OF THE NUN'S PRAYER.

IN the olden time there dwelt in an English convent of the Benedictine rule, a Nun who was filled with virtue, and had great love for Mary Immaculate; and, as she longed exceedingly to have a chapel built in honour of her heavenly Mother, she prayed unceasingly that she might live to see one added to the church.

Many a silent, solitary night she spent

in supplication—making her desire known
to God. Through summer heat and winter
snow she prayed on, always offering the
same petition; and at length a heavenly
voice came to her while she was thus
engaged, bidding her, in God's name,
begin the erection of the Lady Chapel.

Dame Alice thought it but a dream and
took no heed of it, yet before long the same
command was repeated with so much grief
and displeasure sounding in the tones of
that heavenly voice, that she awoke weeping very bitterly, and hastened to her
prioress to tell what had befallen her.

She, also, believed it but a fantastic
dream, and bade the Nun dismiss it from
her mind; but, after a short interval,
Mary herself appeared in vision to Dame
Alice, blaming her so sharply for her
neglect and mistrust that she went again

to the prioress, entreating her with many tears to believe in what she had to tell.

The prioress was touched by her distress, and asked how much she had towards the cost of the chapel.

"Only fifteen pence," replied Dame Alice, casting her eyes upon the ground.

"Then do not fear," said the prioress, "though it be little, our sweet Lady can increase it if she wills, if only your prayers and faith are strong."

So the Nun turned with still more earnest supplication to Heaven, asking that the way of obeying her Blessed Mother's commands might be made known to her, and she was told in revelation that the chapel should be built upon the northern side of the church, in a spot which should be pointed out to her.

It was harvest-time then. The Feast

of the Assumption had just passed, the
earth was gay with flowers, and the sun
shone brightly over all; yet on the morrow, when Dame Alice went to the place described, she found a certain space of ground
covered with snow, which remained from
day-dawn until noon. She was glad at
heart then, and immediately the masons
were sent for, the measurements taken,
and the chapel commenced.

Dame Alice had no store of worldly
wealth, but her faith grew stronger and
stronger, and she redoubled her prayers
to Heaven for means to pay the cost of
this tribute to Mary; and not in vain, for
as each Saturday came round she found
upon the pathway sufficient silver to pay
her workmen—never any more and never
any less—and thus it continued until the
chapel was completed.

There, under a stone leading into the choir, the remains of Dame Alice were interred when she passed away from earth; but for many generations the chapel stood as a memorial of her trustful prayer and fervent love to the Immaculate Mother of God.

LEGEND OF
THE PALM IN THE DESERT.

MANY a legend has been told of that time when Mary and her Holy Child fled into a strange land under the protection of S. Joseph; many a sweet story is known of that weary journey, when the young fair mother clasped her babe in her arms, fearing for Him the hunger and the thirst and the sun's hot gleams.

And thus we hear that one day the Virgin was distressed by the suffering of her little

One, and she said, " Oh, Joseph, what can we do for the Child? If our God will not bestow on us some help surely we shall die in this wild desert."

Fervently she prayed, and as her earnest pleading went up to Heaven, a sound like the trickling of water struck on her ear; and, turning her head to see from whence it came, a stately palm-tree, laden with fruit, rose before her, by whose root ran a clear cool spring of water. But who could reach the fruit so high above their heads, and what had they with which to draw water from the spring? The little Jesus opened His eyes and at His glance the tall tree bent its branches within S. Joseph's reach, and the spring threw up its water like a fountain, clear, and cold, and bright.

Thus were the wayfarers refreshed; even the ass was given some fresh grass which

15 *

sprang up in the dreary desert, at the Will of
Him Who forgetteth no creature which He
has made, while angels hovered around their
Infant Lord and His young Mother.

The Divine Child had gone on His
way; but a fruit He was eating and a drop
of water He left there, brought forth a
growth of fresh herbage on the desert, to
remain for ever.

That day a man was thinking of the promised Messiah, longing, hoping to see Him
Who was the desire of all nations; a man
who was loathsome and horrible even to his
kindred, for he was a leper, and therefore an
outcast.

Yet he was not forgotten of God, for it
had been granted him to see, in vision, the
three holy travellers depart upon their journey, and after that he loved to think he was
following far behind the Mother and Child,

whom he could sometimes behold like a speck upon the distant horizon.

But at length this sight vanished from him, and the soothing hope which had so cheered his heart seemed lost, while the torments of thirst and heat troubled him sorely.

"Ah, could I but see Him, could I but touch the hem of His garment, I should be cleansed," sighed the leper; and falling down upon the shining sand he cried aloud, "Infant Saviour, I believe in Thee, I hope in Thee."

What is before him but a palm-tree and a spring of water?—the very palm and spring which had a while before refreshed his Lord. He rises and struggles on a few more paces, but he cannot reach the water or the fruit, and once again he falls, but this time 'tis upon the green herbage by the stream.

Oh, wonderful mystery! Jesus has rested

there, and that hallowed spot has power to heal. Strength, vigour, new life, animate the leprous form, and purified in heart as by the grace of Baptism, he goes forth whole and well, crying "Praised be God."

LEGEND OF EVESHAM.

AR back in the early ages of the Church in England, there was a desert place all grown over with thorns and briars, which was used as a pasture for the swine belonging to the monastery of Egwin, the third Bishop of Worcester. Four men were employed here every day, one of whom happened to leave his companions and go farther into the thicket than he had ever done before, and to his great amazement he

there beheld a lady standing on a particular
spot of ground, with two maidens of wondrous beauty by her side.   Around the three
there appeared a shining light, far brighter
than the sun, and they were singing sweet
melodies from an open book which the lady
held in her hand.

The rough ignorant man was dazzled by
the splendour of the sight, and went back
to the Bishop, trembling with fear, to tell
what he had beheld.

After prayer and fasting, Egwin was
directed by God to proceed to the thicket
himself; and taking with him three of the
monks, they went towards the valley bare-
foot, and singing psalms and holy hymns.
When they reached the spot to which the
poor swineherd had directed them, the
Bishop left his companions and went alone
into the thicket, where, prostrate on the

ground, he implored God's mercy, and upon rising he beheld the three beautiful virgins exactly as they had been described to him. She who stood between the others was of a surpassing loveliness ; and a sweet fragrance seemed to hover about her, which caused Egwin to believe that she could be no other than the blessed Mother of Christ.   As the thought filled his heart, she blessed him with a golden cross which she held in her hand, and then the vision disappeared, leaving the good Bishop full of peace and consolation.

Before this time he had made a vow to build some church as a thanksgiving, if it should please Almighty God to deliver him from the many trials and persecutions he had been suffering ; and therefore he understood that the Divine Will was, that he should erect a temple in this place and dedicate it to Mary, whose appearance had brought so much joy and comfort to his soul. A spot was cleared, and the pious work immediately commenced; and in later days Evesham became a favourite place of pilgrimage for faithful Christians, who, kneeling there, obtained many graces and gifts through the intercession of the ever-Blessed Mother of God.

LEGEND OF S. BETTELINE.

HE holy hermit S. Betteline is sad and troubled, and he kneels long in prayer to Christ and the Blessed Virgin for help; for by the morrow's sunset he is to leave his quiet solitude upon that green islet, for which he had cast away a crown, that he might watch and pray under the shadow of the Cross.

It is the king who grudges the hermit his cell.

"The Saint has chosen a fair spot," said he; "I warrant me he sleeps well to the murmuring music of the river, and the turf is too soft, the scene too graceful for a hermit. I swear that it shall now be mine."

Then S. Betteline was commanded to prove his right to the ground; and, unless some champion could be found to fight for him in open field, he must on the morrow quit the solitude he loved.

Is there one who will don his armour and draw his sword for Christ? The Saint knows of none such knight, and yet his faith is strong, and thus he prays:

"Lord, if only Thou abide with me, I will not grieve to leave this quiet spot. Barren cliff or flowery meadow are as one to me so that I possess Thee Who art all I need. But for Thy glory's sake abide, and cast down the strength and fury which oppose Thee."

As S. Betteline rose from his knees a sweet calmness filled his soul, and it seemed as if a Divine Voice whispered in his ear,—

"Thy prayer is heard, fear not;" and then he felt neither sorrow nor care, but looked out with a quiet heart upon the peaceful flowing river.

Softly the breeze swayed the willow branches and bent the fragile heads of the wood anemones; but above it rose the sound of a horse's feet approaching, and a man rode up to the narrow door— a stranger to S. Betteline—so slight, so small, that the armour which he wore seemed all too large for him.

"Hermit, I come in the Name of the Blessed Trinity to fight for thee," he

said, and Betteline courteously bent his
head, murmuring,—

"God speed thee; but in Him is all
my trust."

Together they went to the field, where
the King was already seated in pomp and
state, with his courtiers round him, and
a merry shout they raised.

"The hermit hath brought a stout champion, forsooth."

Then the clang of a trumpet echoed
through the forest, and a giant form came
hurriedly onward, seated upon a steed as
black as storm, and he looked at the slight
form of his opponent scornfully, laughing
hoarsely as he wheeled his noble courser
round to begin the affray.

The small frail warrior does not move.
Head, heel, hand, are all still, and his banner
only flutters in the wind, displaying upon

its folds the wrought image of a spotless Lamb and the Holy Cross.

But what ails the giant soldier? The spear shakes in his hand, his steed is checked, for its rider reels and falls to the earth, uttering an awful cry of agony. He had quailed before the glance of that angelic face, and the fair slight form had vanished, too, as the awe-struck whisper passed around,—

"It is S. Michael who has fought the hermit's battle and proved his right to the holy isle; it is S. Michael who has vanquished the fiend with his spear."

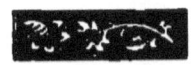

LEGEND OF THE SAN GRAIL.

THE San Grail, or Holy Cup, from which our Blessed Lord drank at His Last Supper had disappeared from the sight of Christians. No more were pilgrims to the altar where it had been kept, rewarded by gazing upon what they longed to see—the sacred relic had mysteriously vanished, and none knew where.

Many a knight searched for the San Grail, seeking by prayer and God's grace to keep heart and conscience free from stain of sin, for well was it known that none might find the Holy Cup who was not in the friendship and favour of the Almighty. Some passed it by unknowingly; but one Sir Galahad was permitted to discover and to recognise the precious treasure which he had so long prayed to behold.

Very early in the morning would he go to visit this Holy Cup, venerating it in remembrance of his Lord, and one day on repairing to the spot he found some one already there; but no earthly visitor was it, for a company of angels surrounded him.

Sir Galahad trembled, and would perchance have drawn back, but the stranger said,

"Come, thou servant of the Lord, and

16

thou shalt see what thou hast so long desired to see. Knowest thou who I am?"

And the knight answered, "Nay."

"I am Joseph of Arimathæa, and the Lord hath sent me here to bear thee company."

Then Sir Galahad lifted his clasped hands to heaven, saying, "Blessed Lord, I thank Thee that Thou hast granted me so great a proof of Thy favour. If it be Thy Will to take me from this world, I pray thee release me, for heavenly joys alone will suffice me now."

As he said these words he knelt down before the Holy Grail, praying fervently to God, and suddenly his soul was carried to heaven by a vast company of angels in the sight of all present. Then a hand from heaven took the sacred vessel and bore it away from earth, and since then human eye hath not looked upon it.

LEGEND OF
THE CHILD IN THE SNOW.

THERE was once a very holy and devout Monk, who had a tender love for the Child Jesus.

One winter's day he had to take a long journey on horseback; and as he passed by a dreary, desolate road, he saw there in the snow a child crying bitterly.

He stopped his horse, for a great compassion filled his heart, and, thinking perhaps the boy had lost his mother, he asked the cause of his tears. But the little child did not answer, and burst out into such deep sobs that the Monk was more than ever sorry for him, and with gentle words entreated him to tell the cause of such great distress.

At length the little one spoke, and said he could not help weeping, for he was perishing from cold and hunger, and there was no one—no one in all the wide world —to take care of him.

The Monk, on hearing this, at once took up the boy in his arms, kissing and comforting him, trying to warm the cold limbs in his close embrace; then he turned to remount his horse, that he might carry his burden to the shelter of some hospice, but in that instant the lovely child had slipped from his arms and vanished. Then the good Monk understood that the little one had been the Most Holy Child Jesus, and he was sad at so great a loss, although his heart turned with thanksgiving to his Divine Lord for the favour He had been pleased to grant him in return for his constant love.

LEGEND OF S. VERONICA.

THE little Veronica from an early age loved Jesus with her whole heart, and in His honour she had erected a small altar in her room, which she adorned with the best flowers she could obtain.

One year, at the approach of Christmas, she prepared her oratory; but there were no flowers ready, and the poor child cried,—

"Ah, how cruel it is that December should refuse me the blossoms I want for

my Lord. I have but dry straw to strew
around His cradle, and that is not enough.
Oh, my God, with Thee it is ever spring-
time. Thou Whose power didst bring forth
all things, canst give me flowers when I
need them."

Then Veronica ran hastily to the garden,
which was all covered with snow, and she
fell upon her knees, and with streaming
eyes, cried,—

"Jesus, Whom I love so much, give me
flowers!"

No blossom pressed upwards through the
frozen snow, but the Lord appeared Himself to the kneeling child.

"Be comforted," He said, "I am the
Flower of the Field, I am the Lily of the
Valley," and then He disappeared.

Veronica wept no more, for she had
recognised Jesus.

"Flower of the Field, Lily of the Valley!" she exclaimed. "Ah, I can need no more."

So the happy child returned to her little room and knelt before her unadorned altar.

"My sorrow has flown," she said. "Amidst the snows of winter I still possess Jesus, and in Him I have the sweetest flowers and the most beautiful fragrance."

LEGEND OF THE TYROLESE BOYS.

TWO little boys were once keeping watch over their father's cows upon the mountains of Tyrol, and towards midday, when the sun was hot and burning, they found that two of the herd had strayed away from the rest. Quickly they started in search of them along the steep narrow mountain paths, but the cattle were not to be seen; and as the hours passed and their labour ·continued vain, they began to shed tears of fear and distress. But the thought of the Blessed Virgin came to one young heart, and the boy begged his brother to kneel down with him and offer some prayers to their Mother in heaven for help in their great trouble.

As they fell upon their knees and invoked the name of Mary, a bright light shone all around them, and a lady of a sweet and gracious countenance appeared close by their side, and in gentle tones bade them wipe away their tears and be consoled, for the two cows had gone home to their stalls. Then, gazing pitifully at the weary children, she added,—" Drink and refresh yourselves, my little ones, for the heat is great and you have wandered far."

"Drink!" cried the boys. "There is no water here, good Mother, else we would gladly take it, for we are thirsty and tired."

As they spoke, the bright vision disappeared, but in the place where she had stood, a clear bubbling stream welled up between the rocks, and the little shepherdlads drank and were refreshed.

It was time then to return homewards with the rest of their herd, so the boys left the spot which seemed to them now so holy; but as they went, they spoke in low and reverent tones of the favour which had been granted them; and though they feared to tell it to their parents and friends, they cherished their secret in their hearts, and never went that way without going to visit the wondrous spring of water, which still continued flowing, saying a prayer there in glory to God and love of His Blessed Mother.

So fifty years passed, and the little lads had grown old—one was so infirm that he

could never leave his home—the other still
watched his herds with the help of a boy
who had been deaf and dumb from his birth.
The lad had often seen the old herdsman
turn aside to visit the miraculous spring,
and kneel and pray there; and at last one
day he also knelt and raised his heart to
God, although he scarce knew why. But
when his master drank of the clear water,
the poor deaf and dumb boy drank too; and
lo! no sooner had it passed his lips than
he could speak as well and plainly as any
other. This miracle could not remain unknown, and many others followed, and
before a year had passed, a chapel, dedicated to the Blessed Virgin, was raised
upon the spot where once the little troubled
shepherd-boys had knelt and told their grief
to that pitiful Mother, and received an
immediate answer to their prayer.

LEGEND OF
THE IDIOT OF FOLGOËT.

N one of the deep forests of Brittany there dwelt a poor idiot named Solomon, but who was, perhaps, better known among the people of the villages round about as "The foolish man of the wood." God, Who had seen fit to deprive this poor creature of the knowledge and understanding which He gives in some measure to nearly all whom He has created, had, however, allowed one ray of light to gleam into the darkness of his mind, and that was the love of the Blessed Virgin. Night and day, amidst the thick growth of trees in the forest, Solomon sung constantly the words " Ave Maria;" and though he was not wise enough to be able to reason and talk about his devotion to this dear Mother, it was evident that he had no thought for anyone else, and his heart was truly consecrated, though unconsciously, to her honour.

The idiot was miserably clad, his feet were bare, he slept upon the earth, resting his head upon some large stone or bit of rock for a pillow, and his only shelter was the branches of the tree under which he made his chief dwelling, close by the stream which flowed through the wood.

Each day poor Solomon went into the town which is on the borders of the wood to beg his bread, using the only words he knew—the "Ave Maria" and "Solomon eats bread." Whatever was given him he accepted thankfully, returning to eat under the shadow of the tree, which was like a little hermitage to him, and, moistening his hard crusts in the water, he would exclaim again and again, "Ave Maria."

In the depth of winter the idiot would plunge up to his chin in the half-frozen stream, singing some Breton rhyme in honour of Mary; and when he became almost numbed from the cold, he regained some slight warmth by swinging to and fro as he held by one of the branches of the tree, saying, "Ave Maria."

With these strange ways it was not surprising that people called him a fool, or mad; little thinking how dear he was to Mary, whom he loved so devotedly.

Once he encountered a band of soldiers,

who shouted, "Who goes there?" upon which he replied, "I am only the servant of the Lady Mary; long live Mary!" and the troop then burst into loud laughter and let him pass by.

Thus, for thirty - nine or forty years Solomon passed his life, and in all that time he had never done an unkindness to any one. At last he became ill, but he sought no better shelter, and the people of that part say that there the Queen of Heaven, with a band of bright angels, visited him, and consoled him with words of loving sweetness.

Thus the poor simple creature died, murmuring with his last breath, "Ave Maria."

He was found lifeless not far from the stream from which he had drunk so often; and his face, which had been so unpleasing and common to the eyes of men, shone in death with a wondrous beauty—that beauty, which was a reflection from the purity of the soul which had but just been set free.

The poor man was buried near by, and the few who had ever known or noticed him, soon forgot him. But it was not God's Will that His humble servant should remain unremembered and unknown, and soon a lily, which no hand had planted, was seen growing upon the spot where Solomon's remains had been laid.

Those who first observed the flower were attracted by its unusual fragrance to draw nearer, and thus it was they found upon each pure white petal the words, "Ave Maria," written in letters of gold.

The news of this miraculous lily soon spread throughout Brittany, and multitudes thronged to the spot that they might see its whiteness and inhale its delicious fragrance,

17

and, above all, gaze upon the golden-lettered
" Ave Maria." Then the poor idiot was
remembered, and the people who had known
him told to visitors the story of his life, and
of his one constant song to his Blessed
Mother.

The ecclesiastics and the nobles of the
land desired to understand more about this
strange man who had lived and died in the
old Breton forest, and accordingly his
remains were sought for. Upon opening
the grave it was found that the fair sweet
lily sprang from the mouth of the poor
despised idiot—that mouth from which no
evil, no unkindly word had ever dropped;
while its root was within his breast, which
had contained no other thought than that
of Mary, the pure and stainless.

Since that time a church, dedicated to
Our Lady, is built upon the spot as a

memorial of the Idiot of Folgoët, who, though so little known or loved on earth, rejoices now among the pure of heart, who see God's face for ever.

THE END.

R. WASHBOURNE PRINTER, 18 PATERNOSTER ROW LONDON.

www.ingramcontent.com/pod-product-compliance
Lightning Source LLC
Chambersburg PA
CBHW020058030726
47498CB00006B/1839